낯선 공간 느낌

On Sense of Strange Spaces

내 삶의 1 % 시간을 품은 런던 서쪽 마을

West London Town linked with 1% in My Lifetime

낯선 공간 느낌 (On Sense of Strange Spaces)
내 삶의 1% 시간을 품은 런던 서쪽마을 (West London Town linked with 1% in My Lifetime)

발 행 | 2021년 6월 1일
저 자 | 박상필
펴낸이 | 한건희
펴낸곳 | 주식회사 부크크
출판사등록 | 2014.07.15.(제2014-16호)
주 소 | 서울특별시 금천구 가산디지털1로 119 SK트윈타워 A동 305호
전 화 | 1670-8316
이메일 | info@bookk.co.kr

ISBN | 979-11-372-4528-0

www.bookk.co.kr
ⓒ 박상필 2021

낯선 공간 느낌
ON SENSE OF STRANGE SPACES

내 삶의 1% 시간을 품은 런던 서쪽 마을
West London Town linked with 1% in My Lifetime

바그사이피르

박상필 朴商必 Sangphil Park

가족과 함께 한 그 느낌들에 대하여

On true senses of being with my family

샴쁘톤 코트 궁과 테즈가 자이 (표지 사진)
Border area between Hampton Court Palace and the Thames River
(including the cover photo)

이 책에 대해 다른 사람이 헤아린 말

"지금껏 그를 가두어 놓았던 낡은 인식세계를 벗어 던지고 새로운 감각을"

도시 산책자 (Flanuer) 박상필은 낯섦을 통해 근원에 대한 질문을 던지며 성찰을 해 나가는 도시 명상가이다. 그의 명상 방식은 엑스타시 (ecstatic) 적이다. 지금껏 그를 가두어 놓았던 낡은 인식세계 (static)를 벗어 던지고 (ec) 새로운 감각을 통해 더욱 더 깊은 알아차림의 세계로 들어간다. 현재의 나를 벗어던진다는 것은 보통 용기가 필요한 것이 아니다. 하지만 그는 이를 담담하게, 그리고 솔직하게 해낸다. 스스로의 감각을 극대화시켜 스스로를, 도시를, 우주를 있는 그대로 보려는 시도를 감행한다. 그리고 그는 새로운 인간으로, 잊고 있었던 원래의 인간으로 재탄생한다. '낯선' 영어로 먼저 쓰고 이를 한글로 번역했다는 저자의 실험에 동참하기 위해 독자들은 영어로 먼저 읽어보길 바란다. 나만 그런 것일까? 오히려 한글보다 영어로 읽을 때 다가오는 울림이 크다. 마치 서비튼 동네 어귀 검은 의자에 저자와 함께 앉아 그의 이야기를 듣는 기분이다. 진실된 자기성찰이 '낯섦'을 통해 드러날 수 있음을 보여준 저자의 노력이 많은 이들에게 전달되기를 바란다.

서현수 건축사

이 책은 경험주의자가 낯선 곳에서 느낀 시간과 공간이 주는 어떤 느낌을 기록한 것이다. 이런 소중한 느낌은 어쩌면 한 공간에서 한 살이에 한번 뿐일지 모른다. 느낌의 실체를 '날줄'과 '판줄'의 작용으로 생각한 들어보지 못한 가설이 놀랍기도 하거니와, 일상 속에서 비 일상을 찾아내고 때로 각성(覺醒)으로 이어지는 느낌의 흐름도 발견할 수 있다. 낯선 곳에 거주할 계획이 있거나, 낯선 곳의 거주가 궁금한 사람들은 마음의 준비를 위해 이 책을 읽어 보기 바란다. 이 책은 보물이다.

황영순 경영학 박사

따뜻한 라디에이터가 있던 방 모퉁이에서
Sitting in the corner of the room with a warm radiator

Discreet comments concerning this book

"His method of looking is therefore genuinely ecstatic in nature"

He considered to be a modern Flanuer in our time sets a new paradigm for contemplating the spatial by embracing 'strangeness.' He lets this 'strangeness' break his status qua. He surrenders himself to be the pure product of it. He courages himself to go out of his 'present' and be in the state of true recognition of who he really is. His method of looking is therefore genuinely ecstatic in nature, by which he opens his eyes and sees things as they really are. What is laid out in this book will surely transform reader's perception toward things in general and inspire to be the road map to urban enlightenment and freedom we need in our time.

H.S Suh, Architect

"Flow of sense concerning non-daily moments in our everyday life"

This book is a unique log of the true sense concerning space and time that the empiricist feels in a strange place. Maybe an exceptional sensation in a strange place will only be once in our lifetime. The unprecedented hypothesis that thinks the truth of sense as the notion of the 'momentome' and the 'fieldome' is surprising. I can find the flow of sensation for extraordinary moments in his daily life. If you plan to live in a strange place or wondering about living in a strange space, read this book and be prepared for help. This book will be your treasure.

Hwang Young Soon, PhD.

Stonehenge connecting heaven and earth, and sheep

리치몬드 공원 꽃밭 집

A cottage in Richmond Park

템즈강 가에서 본 겨울철 햄프튼 코트 궁
Hampton Court Palace in winter seen from the Thames side

가을철 햄프튼 코트 궁의 정원에 있는 분수
Fountain in the garden of Hampton Court Palace in the fall

"스스로에게 묻다"

I ASK MYSELF ABOUT THE WORLD

Wide field grazed by sheep

'나처럼 동네를 떠도는 고양이
A wandering street cat like me

어리둥절한 세상에 있는 나에게

나는 이론가나 비평가가 아니다. 글 잘 짓는 문장가에는 더욱 못 미친다. 있는 그대로의 참 세상을 드러내려는 글 잡이일 뿐이리라. 스스로 여기길 나는 우주를 맴도는 궁금증 많은 나그네이다. 세상은 정말 수수께끼가 차고 넘친다. 얼마 전 내가 다니는 연구원은 일 년이라는 시간과 돈을 들여 곰곰이 생각할 기회를 주었다. 시민의 힘에 바탕을 둔 공공기관이기에 시간과 돈을 아껴야 하는 마음의 내리누름은 오히려 여러 일들[1]을 쫓게 한 모양이다. 낯선 곳에 몸을 두어 모든 걸 처음부터 다시 생각하라는 뜻으로 나는 그 마음의 내리누름을 가라 앉혔다. 이 책에 실은 삼십 편의 글은 세상의 수수께끼에 대해 애 태운 작은 느낌의 조각들이다. 어쩌면 이것들은 나 스스로를 위해 지어 낸 느낌의 허튼 말모이일지 모른다. 낯설기에 영어로 먼저 쓴 뒤 우리말로 바꾸는 게 나 스스로를 발견하는데 더 나으리라는 생각 실험을 해 보았다. 이러하니 고개를 갸우뚱하게 하는 어휘, 흠 있는 문장, 거슬리는 표현, 글 결 파괴 등을 쉽게 찾을 수 있다. 투박한 글 자국들을 만날 때마다 새삼 즐거워지기도 한다. 어리둥절한 세상의 작은 수수께끼를 푼 것처럼.

---

1) '런던의 중심지 재생 경험이 주는 함의'라는 보고서는 2019년에 발행되었다. 이 보고서는 주로 낮에 이루어진 연구 결과인 반면, 이 책에 나오는 글 조각들은 주로 밤에 썼다. 애를 태운 자국들을 버리기 아까워 책으로 묶었다.

To me in a bewildering world

I am neither a theorist nor a critic. Not even a seasoned writer. I'm just an authorling who tries to be honest with myself. I have been thinking for myself I'm a curious wanderer who hovers in the universe for a moment. The world I live in is full of weird riddles. Not long ago, the research institute I work for gave me an opportunity to ponder the mysteries of the world, spending a year of time and money. Since it is a public institution based on the citizens' support, it seems that a lot of work was possible with the pressure to save time.[2] I fixed the vagueness of pressure as the meaning of rethinking everything from the primordial impulses by leaving the familiar and placing my body in a strange place. The thirty essays in this book are tiny pieces of my life about the mystery of the world.

---

[2] The most basic research report, 'Implications of the Regeneration Experience in the London central areas,' was published in 2019. While the report is the result of daytime research, this book, with 30 essays, is a collection of small pieces written before falling asleep against the backdrop of a night in west London. I put them in one book because I was sorry to throw them away.

These are the wild pieces of my personal documentary I wrote down myself. Since I lived in a strange space, I experimented with the idea that writing in awkward English first and translating it into familiar Korean would help me find myself more. Therefore, it is easy to find somewhat awkward vocabulary, incomplete sentences, ambiguous expressions, and context destruction. Whenever I find clumsy writing marks one by one, I get refreshed with strange joys. Such as solving the world's mystery.

"기억 이미지는 한번 말로 고정되면 지워지지." 폴로는 말했다. "나는 베니스를 한꺼번에 모두 잃는 게 두려워. 만약 내가 베니스에 대해 말한다면 나는 이미 조금씩 베니스를 잃는 거야"

"Memory's images, once they are fixed in words, are erased," Polo said. "Perhaps I am afraid of losing Venice all at once, if I speak of it, or perhaps, speaking of other cities, I have already lost it, little by little." Italo Calvino, *Invisible Cities*. 2017.

햄프턴 코트 궁 정원에서
In the Hampton Court Palace

낯선 느낌에 대해서

'낯섦'은 처음과 끝의 경험이 이어진 시공간에 얽힌 이야기이다. 나는 런던에 도착한 2018년 1월 2일부터 부산에 돌아온 12월 28일까지 런던 서부지역인 킹스턴의 서비튼이라는 작은 마을에서 경험했던 낯선 공간3)의 날 느낌을 글로 드러내려 했다. 떠다니는 환상과 사전 앎 없이 마음을 모양 짓는데 영향을 주는 몸을 어떤 시간과 공간에 내 놓으면 몸에 무언가가 계속 이는데 나는 이 모든 것을 '참 느낌 (超越感, Metasense)'이라는 우리말에 담아 보려 했다. 누군가는 '참 느낌'이라는 말을 바꾸어 '영감 (靈感)', '감성 (感性)', '지각 (知覺)' 등을 내놓을 수 있겠지만 그 어떤 것도 넉넉하지 않다고 생각한다. 여기에서 다룬 이 느낌의 뜻은 이것들을 아우르는 보다 큰 관념이다. 영어단어인 '메타센스(Metasense)'의 원래 뜻은 둘레 환경을 스스로 알아차리는 반성과 배움을 아우르는 말이기 때문에 고민 끝에 '참 느낌'과 짝지었다. 물론 내가 생각하는 이 느낌은 사전에서 나오는 뜻 이상이다.

---

3) 내가 산 곳은 템즈 강 서쪽인 킹스턴 중심지의 작은 마을인 서비튼이라고 불리는 곳이다. 여기는 강과 이어진 오랜 역사를 간직한 마을이다. 중세 시대까지 거슬러 올라간다. 나는 내가 몸담고 있는 부산연구원에서 해외 연수 프로그램에 의해 이곳에 오게 되었다. 여기는 나에게 완전히 낯선 곳이었다. 바쁜 탓에 미리 준비 없이 오게 되었으니 그 낯섦은 더할 나위 없다.

내 스스로를 곰곰이 살펴보니 이 '느낌'은 '날줄(Momentome)⁴'과 '판줄(Fieldome)⁵'로 이루어진 것 같다. 이 '날줄'과 '판줄'에 대한 관념은 삼십 편의 글을 다시 읽으면서 나 스스로 모양 지은 말이다. 모호한 날이 흐릿한 판과 이리 저리 얽히고 포개지면서 모양 짓기 어려운 어떤 느낌이 생기는 듯하다. 날은 너무 빠르게 지나가고 판은 너무 작기에 그 느낌을 제대로 알아채기는 힘들다. 만약 내가 내 몸 안쪽의 영적 우주에 제대로 힘을 쏟아 붓지 않는다면 바로 지루함 혹은 헛것에 빠져 허우적거리게 될지 모른다. 한번 지나간 그 '날줄'과 그 '판줄'은 다시 돌아오지 않는다.

나는 '참 느낌'을 말이라는 도구 상자로 드러내기 어렵다고 생각한다. 도구 상자가 작으면 더욱 그러하리라. 그림과 사진도 마찬가지이다. 그것은 세상과 몸이 만나서 생기는 수수께끼를 나에게 계속 던질 뿐이다. '날줄'과 '판줄'을 말, 그림, 사진 등으로 드러내려는 내리누름은 뜻의 과잉을 만들고 기억의 형질도 바꾸는 듯하다. 외국 땅이라는 이유를 들어 비록 서툴지만 영어로 그 느낌을 먼저 드러내고 한글로 바꾸어 보았지만 말의

---

4) 내가 알아차릴 수 있는 가장 작은 시간 단위로 생각했다. 작지만 무궁무진한 이야기가 서로 얽혀 있는 쪼개진 시간의 묶음을 뜻한다. 홀로 있지 않고 '판줄'과 함께 움직이는 듯하다.
5) 시간에 대한 '날줄' 관념처럼 내가 알아차릴 수 있는 가장 작은 공간 단위로 생각했다. 가장 작지만 무궁무진한 이야기의 무대가 서로 얽혀 있는 쪼개진 공간 묶음을 뜻한다. '날줄'과 짝지어 움직이는 듯하다.

도구 상자가 작기에 그 느낌은 더욱 희미해지고 만다. 이렇게 보면 여기에 남긴 삼십 편의 느낌 이야기는 동화처럼 꾸며진 말잔치일지 모른다. 허술한 말을 통해 이루어진 뜻은 환상과 이어지기 쉽다. 어쩌면 말은 끝없는 상상 혹은 환상을 불러일으키는 천사 혹은 악마의 마법 상자일지도 모른다. 이것을 깨닫는 순간, 나는 입을 막고 '날줄'과 '판줄'이 추는 춤사위의 낯선 느낌을 그대로 품어야만 한다.

On Strange Senses

The 'strangeness' of something would be an experimental story concerning time and space connecting the starting point and the endpoint that I met with it. Until I arrived at a small town called Surbiton in the Kingston-upon-Thames borough, London, on January 2nd, 2018, and returned to Busan on December 28th, 2018, I tried to honestly express the sense of the strange space[6] that I

---

6) I lived in Surbiton, a small town in the Kingston region of the upper Thames. The Surbiton, with a long history that dates back to the Middle Ages, is connected to the River Thames. I came this through an overseas training program at the Busan Development Research Institute, where I am working. The Surbiton is an extraordinary place to me.

experienced around the Surbiton area. When I put my body into a reality that influences the mind's form without any fixed illusions in a strange time and space without any prior knowledge, everything that touches my body is revealed by 'true sense (used interchangeably with the word, metasense).' I think that someone could suggest 'inspiration,' 'sensibility,' and 'perception,' but none of them were enough for me. The meaning of 'metasense' covered here is a more significant notion encompassing these. The original purpose of the English word 'metasense' is a word that includes the reflection to be aware of the surrounding environment and the ability to learn, so after careful consideration, I match it with the Korean 'Cham Neucqim,' Of course, the 'metasense' that I think of is more than the meaning of sense in the dictionary.

From what I have looked carefully at myself, the true sense seems to be made up of 'momentome (Naljul in Korean)[7]' and

---

Since I came without prior preparation, the strangeness was perfect.

7) I assume that it is the smallest unit of time that I can perceive. It is the smallest, but it means the bundle of divided times when moments of an endless story are entangled.

'fieldome (Panjul in Korean)[8].' The new notion of the 'momentome' and the 'fieldome' is what I came up with because I couldn't find the right word while re-reading 30 essays. It seems that ambiguous something like something difficult to shape concerning a sense arises as the fuzzy moment entangles and superposes onto the blurred field. The moments pass so fast, and the field is so tiny that it is difficult to recognize the sense properly. If I don't correctly fall into the spiritual universe inside my body, I'll quickly fall into wearisomeness or fantasy. The 'momentome' and the 'fieldome' which have passed once do not return to them.

I am sure the 'metasense' is difficult to reveal with a small toolbox called the system of words. It is even more so if the toolbox is small like mine. The same goes for pictures and photos. It throws at me an unknown mystery that arises when

---

8) I assume that it is the smallest unit of space that I can perceive. It is the smallest, but it means the bundle of divided spaces in which endless story stages are entangled.

the world and the body meet. The pressure to reveal the 'momentome' and the 'fieldtome' in words, pictures, and photos seems to create an excess of meaning and distort memory traits. Although I am clumsy because this is a foreign land, I tried to reveal the ambiguous sense in English and then convert it into Korean, but the toolbox for words is small, so the ' true sense' is often more distorted. In this way, all of the 30 essays left here may be an arrangement of words decorated like a fairy tale. The meaning formed through vulgar words is connected to my fantasia. The terms may be the magic box of angels or the devil that unleashes endless imagination or fantasy. As soon as I realize this, I have to close my mouth and accept the body's strange sense created by the relationship between the 'momentome' and the 'fieldome.'

January 2021

'참 느낌'은 '날줄'과 '판줄'의 관계로 이루어진 어떤 것이 아닐까? (위 그림)
Is the reality of true sense something concerning the relationship between
the 'momentome (Naljul in Korean)' and the 'fieldome (Panjul' in Korean)' ?

'날줄'과 '판줄'을 가둔 런던 공간형태 (하양은 건물· 검정은 빈 곳, 다음 쪽)
The urban spatial form shaping the 'momentome (Naljul in Korean)' and
the 'fieldome (Panjul' in Korean)' of London life

Note: White is a built-up area and black is an empty area (the next page)
Source: Sangphil, Park (2019), Implication of urban regeneration experiences in Lonon central areas, BDI

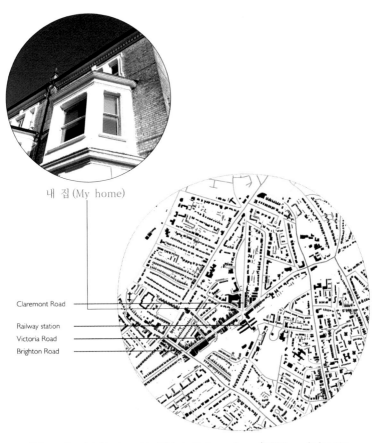

내 집 (My home)

Claremont Road
Railway station
Victoria Road
Brighton Road

일 년 즘 산 런던 킹스턴, 서비튼 지역의 그림-바탕 지도

Figure-ground map of the Surbiton of Kingston, London I lived in for about a year

Note : 반지름 2km인 원이 이루는 범위 (The area formed by a circle with a radius of 2km)
Source: Ilkka Torma and Sam Griffiths, 2017. High Street Changeability: The Effect of Urban Form on
Demolition, Modification and Use Change in Two South London Suburbs. Urban Morphology: 11.

'날줄'과 '판줄'을 자유롭게 하는 열린 장소 (앞 쪽 그림)

Open place to make the 'momentome' and the 'fieldome' free (the previous side)

Note : 그리니치 공원에서 본 '여왕의 집' 모습 (View of Queens House from Greenwich Park)

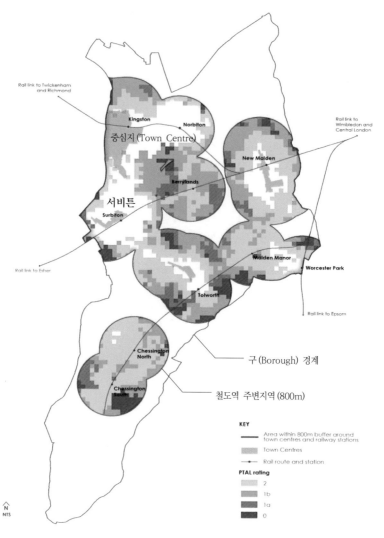

서비튼 마을 위치
Location of Surbiton in Kingston, London

Note : 서비튼 마을은 런던광역시 킹스턴-어폰-템즈 구(自治區)의 서측에 있고 템즈 강에 맞닿음 (The neighborhood of Surbiton is
        located on the west side of Kingston-upon-Thames borough, London, and is connected to the upper Thames River)
Source: London Datastore (런던광역시 홈페이지에 있는 자료방)

"낯섦을 느끼다"

I SENSE COUNTLESS STRANGENESS

템즈강 여왕산책로에 있는 벤치
Bench on the Queen's Promenade by the River Thames

18   하늘을 향해 뻗어 있는 가로수 나뭇가지 (템즈강 가는 길)
Branches of trees stretching toward the sky (The way to the Thames)

집을 잠시 비우는 날

언제부터였을까? 나는 늘 어디론가 떠나고 싶었다. 떠올리니 아주 어릴 적부터이다. 늘 고향과 멀어지고픈 바람. 뚜렷한 까닭은 모른 채. 나는 그저 자연스러운 강 흐름처럼 살고 싶었다. 아이 같은 이 버릇은 계속 이어졌다. 그렇다고 고향을 정말 떠날 수는 없었다. 떠날 때마다 또 다른 고향이 곁에 다시 돋아났다. 언제부터인지 몰라도 나는 바꾸기로 다짐했다. 고향을 떠나기보다 살피기로. 오늘, 그러려고 떠난다. 아주 멀리.

해가 떠오르고 있다. TV 소리가 밤새 어지러웠다. 묵은 이야기들을 털기 위한 들썩거림이었으리라. 나도 풀어보려 한다. 실이 몸과 마음을 감고 있는 듯. 몸과 달리 마음이 실타래이다. 자꾸만 풀어져 내려앉는다, 마음이 몸을 보챈다.

비행기가 꿈틀거린다. 실이 풀리기 시작한다. 멀리 있을 또 다른 집을 바라본다. 내 인생의 1% 즈음인 이 시간 속 첫발을 내디딘다. 내 발걸음을 담은 비행기는 하늘로 솟는다. 나를 품을 시공간이 기다리고 있다. 흔들리는 의자에 머리를 붙이고 눈을 감는다. 마음의 실을 다시 세게 감는다. 곧 낯선 새 집에 실을 내려야 한다. 마음이 잔잔해진다.

"사람들은 도시에서 살면 안 되는 거였어. 그들은 무서워서 함께 모였고, 그렇게 사는 게 그들을 점점 더 두렵게 만들었을 뿐이야."

"People were never supposed to live in cities. They gathered together since they were scared and then living like that only made them more and more afraid." Peter Rock, *My Abandonment*, 2018.

비행기 안에서 내려다 본 런던
London overlooking from the plane

The day leaving away from my home for a while

Since when did I start it? It is something about my home. I always wanted to leave somewhere, and I am still doing it now. Come to think of it, I have done it from childhood to adulthood. When I was young, my wish was to leave my home. There is no apparent reason or goal. I just wanted to live like a natural stream of the river without stopping moments. The immature habit hasn't disappeared after I become an adult. But I have never left my home. Strangely, a new home always has been beside me. Although I left my home and arrived anywhere, surprisingly, another my house always had been there. From a vague moment, I don't know when it started, but I changed my mind to exploration without leaving my home. Today, I will go out to explore strange spaces. Now I will go a long way.

The sun is rising. During last night, TV sounds were noisy. These look like a clamor to forget the old story. I have to clear out my body and mind. My brain has to be filled with something. My body and mind seem to be tightly tied by threads. My body is flying, but my mind is sinking. My mind on the land seems to pull my body.

The airplane with me is moving and flying. The thread that binds me begins to loosen. I am going to another home after passing long distance. New time in there will account for about 1% of my life. I put forward the first foot. The airplane, with my walking foot, goes through the sky. Maybe the time in the home ought to be waiting for me. I sit down in a chair and close my eyes. The thread bundle of my mind tightly seems to tie my body. Soon, I have to loosen a piece of the thread bunch into the home. My heart is becoming calm.

1st January

처음 런던에 도착하여 이틀간 머무른 동네
The neighborhood where I arrived in London and stayed there for two days

집 방 모퉁이 의자
A chair in the corner of the room

왠지, 귀한 집 열쇠

집 셋돈이 다달이 이백삼십만 원. 오호통재라! 이 것 저 것 세가 붙으니 다달이 삼백만원이다. 백 년 전 즘 지어진 노동자 집이라니. 오래 잘 쓰면 비싸지는 모양. 두툼한 집 설명서에 땀을 빼며 문간에 홀로 서있던 그 날이 또렷하다. 어릴 적에는 자물 쇠 따위를 모를 만큼 정이 도타운 작은 시골 마을에 살았다. 그 때 뿐이지, 뒤에 도시 삶에서는 주로 단추를 눌러 열었다. 이러니 어쩔 줄 모를 수밖에. 엊그제까지 그리하지 않았던가. 쇠뭉치를 손에 움켜쥐니 낯선 느낌이 힘줄을 타고 온 몸에 퍼진다. 갑자기 문을 여는 쇠와 단추의 다름이 궁금하다. 돌리느냐 누르느냐 그게 물음이로다.

런던에 다다른 지 사흘 째. 스스로 문 여는 첫 날. 조심스레 문구멍에 쇠를 밀어 넣었다. 잘 들어가지 않는다. 자물 통에 겨우 쇠를 밀어 넣은 뒤, 힘을 주어 보았다. 꼼짝하지 않는다. 여러 번 해 보았지만 마찬가지. 자물 통을 째려보는 사이, 땀방울이 이마에 맺히고 있었다. 찬 공기가 땀방울을 식힐 무렵, 뜻밖에 이웃의 도움으로 집에 겨우 들어갈 수 있었다. 금 빛 머리칼과 푸른 눈동자를 한 소녀의 친절. 스스로 문을 연 건 나중 일이다.

그 뭉치에는 여러 쇠들이 있다. 쇠마다 스스로의 쓸모가 있다. 그 쓸모에 의해서 집에 들락거릴 수 있다. 만약 쇠가 없거나 어디 있는지 모르면 집에 들 수 없다. 만약 쇠가 세상에 하나뿐이거나 다시 만들 수 없다면 집에 들어갈 수 없을 거라. 이층에 있는 집에 들려면 나는 네 개의 낯선 쇠 구멍을 지나야 한다. 얼마나 지나야 이 낯섦에 익숙해질까? 움직일 때마다 바지 호주머니 속에서 쇠들이 달그랑달그랑 거린다.

Somehow, just treasured house keys

I rented a small house with a monthly rent of over 2.3 million won, a worker's flat made about a hundred years ago. Alas ! It is almost 3 million won (2,000 £) each month when the council tax is added for this and that. I guess the well-managed old house is expensive. I distinctly remember the day when I was standing alone in front of my rental house. A moment ago, I received a bundle of the door keys for our home that my family has to live in for a year from a real estate staff in Surbiton, London. When I was a child, I lived in a rural neighborhood where trust in my neighbors was so high that I didn't even need a key. After living in the city, because I haven't used the house keys for about thirty years, it was natural that I was embarrassed by the access. Before coming here, I opened the door using my finger to push my house's key button. So, if someone knows the key numbers of my house, they always will be able to open the door and enter my home. As I grasped the bundle of keys in one hand, a strange feeling spreads throughout the body through the tendon. I wonder what the difference between the key and the button. That is the question of whether I turn or press it.

It was the third day of my arrival in London. On that day, I intended to try to open the door of my house. I pushed the key carefully through the door keyhole, but I felt the key not go in well. As I tried to open it, the key didn't turn. I tried a few times, but it was the same. As I glanced at the door with the lock, beads of sweat were forming on my forehead. By the time the chilly air was cooling the sweat drops on my forehead, fortunately, I was able to enter the house thanks to my neighbor's help. With the help of a neighbor, I could barely enter my home. The kindness of a girl with golden hair and blue pupils. It was later that I opened the door myself.

There are various keys in the bundle. Each key has its purpose. By the purpose of the key, I can enter into a home or can't. If I haven't the key or don't know where it is, I can't enter into my house forever. If the key is the only one in the world, or if no one can make it again, I will be unable to enter into my home. To arrive at my house on the second floor, I have to go through four strange keyholes. How long before my body gets used to this strangeness? Every time I move, the keys dangle in my pants pocket.

27th January

In front of the house where a worker lived a hundred years ago

일 년 사이 머문 집
A home for my family for a year

주변을 두리번거리며 거니는 거리

여기에 온 지 얼마 안 되었을 때. 점심끼니를 치운 뒤, 나는 빅토리아 거리를 거닐고 있었다. 답답했던가? 그냥 쭉 뻗은 길 따라 걷고 싶어졌다. 길옆에 나란히 붙어 가지런한 가게들을 구경하면서. 길을 거니는 동안, 나는 길 건너기에 앞서 이리저리 두리번거리고 있음을 알아차렸다. 나는 그 낯선 몸짓이 언제 만들어졌는지 모른다.

이제 집 가까이 여러 길을 안다. 초승달 모양의 공원에 가려면 길 몇 개를 지날 지도 안다. 길을 건너려면 나는 늘 날카롭다. 차에 치일 수 있기 때문. 아직 그런 적 없지만. 머리가 흐려지면 종종 템즈 강 옆길을 거닌다. 여왕 산책로라 불리는 길. 거길 가려 길을 건너려면 나는 자꾸만 두리번거린다. 아마 자동 몸짓이리라. 나는 다람쥐처럼 재빨리 길을 건넌다.

나와 달리 여기 사람들은 길을 건너며 두리번대지 않는다. 그들은 정지선 앞에 기다리는 운전자에게 손을 들어 미소 짓는다. 따라해 보지만 조금 뒤 나는 다시 두리번댄다. 어릴 적 나는 그러지 않았는데. 이 몸짓은 우악스러운 편의주의에 근거한 보이지 않는 규칙에 의해 유도되었을지 모른다. 목에 힘을 잔뜩 준 나는 길 보도 끝에 다시 선다.

가지런한 킹스턴에 있는 거리
The neat street in Kingston area

Streets walking along gazing around

It was not long after I arrived here. After lunch, I was looking around Victoria Street by Surbiton station. Was it because I felt frustrated? I wanted to walk along the road, which had the axis of a perspective view. Looking at the small shops arranged side by side by side of the road. By the way, while I strolled aimlessly along the street, I had perceived a habit that I have of constantly raising my head and looking right and left nervously before I cross the street. I don't know when that gesticulation was formed in me.

Now I know the many roads around my house, and I know how many roads I have to cross when I go to the Crescent Park, and I'm always careful when I cross the roads because I might bump into a car. Until now, I've never been threatened by cars. And I often walk along the street by the Thames in my incredible moments. It is called the Queen's Promenade. While I go there, I continuously look around as I cross the roads. It seems to be such a habit that I do it automatically, without thinking. I quickly cross them like a squirrel.

Unlike me, I notice that other Surbitoners don't continuously look around as they cross the roads. They raise a hand and smile at drivers who stay before the signal line on the streets. I intentionally try to follow their expressions but I realize that I automatically look around again after a moment. When I was very young, I never did so. The little habit on the street may be induced by invisible rules based on the expediency of belignorant person. I apply a strain to my neck muscles and I stand again at the end of the sidewalk on the road.

6th February

여왕산책로 가는 길
The street to Queen's promenade

얼룩말 횡단보도를 걷는 사람들
People walking across a zebra crosswalk

창밖에 펼쳐진 변덕꾸러기 같은 날씨

어떤 건 나를 늘 깨게 한다. 날씨는 어김없이 오늘도 내 몸과 마음을 흔들어 댄다. 실없이 놀리는 듯하다. 오늘 또 날씨에 속는다. 요즘 나는 이곳 날씨 변덕과 실랑이 중이다. 해가 나는가 하면 구름이 차고 비가 오는가 하면 해가 든다. 꾼 꿈을 깨고 금새 새 꿈을 꾸게 한다. 날씨는 감성과 이성을 이리저리 굴린다. 참으로 희한한 장난꾸러기이다.

날씨는 눈치 밖에 있다. 안에 영근 꿈을 괴롭힌다. 창밖을 보니, 잿빛 하늘에 나뭇잎이 춤춘다. 바람이 놀러 온 마냥 작은 잎들이 이리저리 흔들거린다. 여린 나뭇가지들이 손짓한다. 홀리는 모양이다. 다람쥐도 꼬리를 흔들며 나무를 오르내린다. 친구처럼 함께 춤춘다. 오늘 나의 마음이 나뭇가지에 보챈다. 내 꿈이 다람쥐 꼬리 끝에 매달려 함께 휘청거린다.

쉬어야 한다. 내 바람을 모른 척, 날 바람이 나무에 다시 손짓한다. 나를 다시 꼬드긴다. 흔들리지 말아야 한다. 다짐하는 순간 하늘이 더 흐리다. 갑자기 물 몇 방울이 창을 때린다. 나무에 걸린 꿈 방울이 터져 어딘가로 사라진다. 의자에 털썩 기댄다. 꿈을 다시 그려야 한다. 내 순간은 날씨에 달려있다. 어이없이 어김없다. 날씨는 매순간 나의 감성과 이성을 함께 흔들어 깨운다. 날씨는 말 뜻대로 내 날 모습 뒤에 선다.

번덕꾸러기처럼 배배꼬인 계단 난간

A twisted stair rail like a creature of moods

The weather outside the window as a creature of moods

Something constantly keeps me awake. The weather shakes my body and mind. I guess that it is always controlling me. Recently, I have struggled with the change of the weather in Surbiton, London. Today I have been created by the weather. The sun disappears as it shines. And the sun shines as the rainfall down. So I have withdrawn my plan and again have to make a new plan compatible with the weather. It is curiously that the weather shakes sensibility as well as reason. It makes my plans to be useless things. It is slyboots.

I am thinking about what I will do today. When I look out of the window in my house, tree leaves are dancing in the grey sky. An invisible wind seems to come to play with the tree. Many leaves bump against each other. Tree branches seem to peeve at me. A squirrel runs up and down the tree, and then it seems to play with the tree branches too. Today, my dream in the plan is shaking with the tree branches.

The weather keeps pushing my body and mind. Whether big or small, I think that what to do right now depends on the weather. Suddenly It is again raining from the grey sky. I had to fold my plan that I had a moment ago. So my little dream in the project to stroll disappears too. I again sit on a chair. I will have to make a plan. Maybe the weather will again shake my sensibility and reason from moment to moment. Change of the weather will drive me into remarkable experiences in this place.

30th April

비온 뒤, 갠 날씨
A walk in the sun after the rain.

A walk under the cloud before the rain

세상 속에 빛나는 불 꽃 같은 들풀

이 첫 느낌을 뭐라 해야 할까? 참 날카롭게 추운 날. 찬 바람이 뇌 세포 고리에 배어들었다. 여기 온 지 열흘이 채 안 되었을 때. 추위 속 밖에서 나는 언 땅에 뿌리내린 친근한 들풀을 찾아냈다. 밤하늘에 빛나는 샛별처럼 힘 찬 잎을 편 그것을 또렷이 기억한다. 모양과 색깔로 냉이일지 모른다고 여겼다. 그러나 나는 틀림없이 틀리고 말았다. 그 들풀 이름은 민들레였다. 한참 뒤 꽃이 피고서야 알았다. 민들레는 참을 드러내려 오래 버티었다. 문 둘레에 끈질기게 피는 꽃 !

내 집 가까이 열린 공간에는 들풀이 가지각색이다. 마을 곳곳을 거닐 때면 이름 없는 들풀과 자주 마주치곤 한다. 그것들은 어디서나 살고 심지어 좁은 틈에서도 산다. 갈라진 작은 바위 틈에도 있다. 그것은 겨울 찬 바람을 이겨낸 열정의 불꽃이다. 아마도 그 생명력은 하루 만에 이루어진 게 아닐 게다. 서비튼은 사람의 활동이 가득한 마을이자 들풀의 활력이 가득한 풀밭이기도 하다.

어떤 사람이 두고 간 창 밖 항아리 속 풀을 본다. 그것들은 이름을 가졌겠지만 나는 모른다. 적어도 이름 없는 들풀에 이름이라도 지어주자. 나

만의. 잠시 그 들풀의 삶의 역사를 생각한 후, '세상 속 불 꽃'이라 부르기로 했다. 우리가 꽃이라 부르며 사랑스러워하는 풀도 처음에는 이름 모를 들풀이었다. 세상은 낯선 것들로 가득한 게다. 가만히 생각하니 이 세상은 무엇 하나 뚜렷하지 않다. 아마도 나는 마지막 숨을 거둘 때까지 이 세상을 헤매며 두리번거리는 학습자이리라. 푸른 들풀처럼 살다가, 흙에 달라붙은 누르께한 잎처럼 수그러들더라도. 그렇게.

Wild herbs like flames shining in the world

What can I express this strange sense? A sharply chilly day. A cold wind was permeating into the chain of neurons in my brain. It was less than ten days since I was here. When I was outside in the cold, I found a familiar weed rooted in the frozen ground. I vividly remember the spreading leaves of the vibrant weed like a lighting morning star in the night. When I saw its shape and color at that time, I guessed that it might be a shepherd's purse. But it was definitely wrong. Its name was a dandelion. Long after,

I knew it for sure only after the flower bloomed. The dandelion held on for a long time, revealing the truth. Flowers that blooms vitally around the door (or question)?

There are various weeds in open spaces around my house. Whenever I walk along the street in my neighborhood, I quickly find the unnamed weeds. They are living everywhere and even live in the narrow crack between pavements. They also live in a tiny cleft in the rocks. Maybe it is the flames of passion ignited by the fact that they have got over a cold wind during the winter. Perhaps, the vitality of the weeds has not been built in a day. In some ways, Surbiton is the town full of people's activity and the sward full of weed's vitality. The world I live in is vague.

As I look out the window, I also see some weeds that grow up in the pots that someone has left. Although the weeds in the pots each may have names, I don't know all their words. At the very least, I have to try to name the unnamed weeds for myself. After I imagine the life history of the weeds for a while,

I decided to call the weeds 'Flames in the World'. Many plants we call flowers and love were originally just weeds that did not know their names. It seems to be evident that the world is filled with strange things. Therefore, Perhaps I am a wandering learner who must continue to explore the world until the last breath. Even if I live like a vivid grass now, I will later wither like sallow leaves clinging to the land. I will do so.

10th June

생이로 착각한 봄날, 민들레
A dandelion like shepherd's purse

뒤죽박죽 속 음식 잔치

우습지만, 지금 배가 부른지 고픈지 모른다. 머핀에 손이 간다. 배가 고픈 걸까? 꿀꺽 삼킨다. 달다. 배가 부르지만 고프기도 하다. 나는 줄곧 굶주린 나그네이다. 텁텁한 막걸리, 새콤한 도토리 무침, 쫄깃한 비빔 밀면, 시큼한 파절이, 고소한 양념통닭, 총각김치 등이 떠오른다. 산허리에서 굽던 찰진 고깃살까지 부른다. 이 배부름과 배고픔 사이의 헷갈림은 어디에서 오는가?

배부름 마비인가 배고픔 중독인가? 깨자. 세게 발버둥 쳐보자. 마비 혹은 중독 탓일지 모른다. 어쩌면 자연에서 온 무엇인가와 이어졌다. 음식에 얽힌 기억일 수도 있다. 무엇 때문일까? 나는 자연 속 무엇이 이렇게 만드는지 잘 모른다. 낯선 음식 탓이겠지만 이제는 어느 정도 익숙할 법도 한데 입과 배 안의 장기 세포들은 여전히 음식이 낯선가 보다.

음식은 자연에서 왔음을 새삼 깨닫는다. 자연은 인간이 먹는 음식인가? 인간은 자연이 먹는 음식인가? 나는 계속 먹어 왔고 앞으로도 그렇다. 생물로 만든 덤덤한 샌드위치, 돼지를 구운 쫄깃한 고기, 동물 젖에서 나온 구수한 치즈, 토마토 주스를 끓여 부은 새콤한 파스타 맛을 느낀다. 또 다른 마비 혹은 중독인가? 아니면 확장인가? 재밌게도 머핀에 손을 다시 뻗는다.

러셀이 살던 집 뒤뜰에서 먹은 빵과 홍차
Bread and black tea in the backyard of Russell's house

A funny food party in a muddle

Funny, but my hands move for a muffin to eat. It is as if I have a beast in my stomach. I put and chew it in my mouth and then swallow it at a gulp. It is a very sugary taste. It goes away somewhere inside me. I am confused by something. Even if I am full, I still seem to be hungry. I am like a starving traveler. In my mind, I recall some food. There are dry rice wine, sweet and sour acorn jelly salad, chewy wheat noodles, sour leek salad, fried chicken in sweet sauce, radish kimchi, and so on. Later, I even recalled the moment when I ate grilled beef at a mountainside. Where ever does the confusion between the fullness and the hunger come from?

Is it the inability to be full or the addiction of hunger? I have to awaken myself. I have to try to solve the confusion. I think that clues to the confusion are connected to the inability or the addiction. Maybe it relates to the something of ingredients. Otherwise, is it related to memories of food? What on earth is its origin? I don't know what in nature causes me to fall into the inability or the addiction? All of this may be attributed to unfamiliar food, but it seems to be familiar to some extent now, but the organ cells in the mouth and stomach still seem to feel strange.

I am earnestly thinking about all food gathered in nature. Is all of nature the food of humans? Otherwise, is the human the food of nature? Obviously, I ate in the past, am eating now, and will eat foods in the future. I seem to feel the taste of light sandwiches made from various living things, chewy steak from pork, savory cheese from animal milk, and sweet pasta with boiled tomato juice. Is this another symptom of human history? Is this the extension of the signs of inability or addiction? Funny, and I stretch my arm back toward the muffin.

큰 **풍선**을 불고 터뜨리는 신 느낌

얼마 전 다른 고향으로 떠난 스티븐 호킹 박사는 그 책, '시간의 역사 간추림 (A Brief History of Time)'에서 우리는 어리둥절한 세상에 있는 스스로를 뜻하지 않게 알아차린다고 했지. 그 생각이 맞다. 나는 어리둥절한 세상에 살고 있다. 나는 우주로 불리는 세상이 본바탕을 알 수 없는 풍선 같다고 상상하곤 한다. 어쩌다 풍선이 커지면 터져 사라지지만 거꾸로 작아지면 쪼그라져 가라앉을 게다. 누군가는 알맞게 이 풍선에 바람을 계속 불어 넣어야 한다. 누가 그 누군가인가? 혹은 무엇인가?

나는 어리둥절한 가장자리에 늘 서 있다. 그 자리는 세상과 나를 가르는 상상이 빚은 선이다. 거기에는 시간과 공간이 함께 있다. 내 집 가까이 있는 거리, 광장, 공원 등을 둘러 걷곤 한다. 나는 그 곳에 홀로 있을 때마다 스스로 세상 가장자리에 서 있다고 느낀다. 때때로 나는 그 자리 너머인 다른 세상을 상상한다.

나는 생각한다. 세상은 있는 모든 것이다. 모든 곳과 때에 있는 모든 것을 알지는 못한다. 그 모든 것을 느낄 수조차 없다. 다른 사람들도 마찬가지이다. 누군가 혹은 무엇에 의해 그 가장자리에 있는 풍선이 유지되고 있는가? 아마 어느 날 나는 그 세상 가장자리 너머를 여행할 것이다. 그 경계 너머 어딘가에 신이 있을지 모른다. 참으로 알 수 없는 노릇이다. 정말 웃기다.

God blowing and bursting a giant balloon

'We find ourselves in a bewildering world,' as Dr. Stephen William Hawking, who had gone to another home world a while ago, said this in his book 'A Brief History of Time'. I think his thought is proper. I am living in a bewildering world. Sometimes, I imagine that the world is a balloon called the universe that nobody knows it. Somehow, If the balloon gets too big, it will burst with a popping sound and suddenly disappear. In adverse, if the balloon gets too small, it will shrink and sink. Someone has to inflate the balloon appropriately and do the duty periodically. Who is that someone? Or what is it?

I think that I am always standing on a bewildering boundary, an imaginary line that separates the world and me. In there, there are time and space together. I walk around the spaces like streets, neighborhood squares, parks, etc., near my home. Whenever I am alone in the places, I feel myself standing on the boundary of the world. Sometimes I imagine another world beyond the border.

I think that the world is everything that exists. But I don't know what everything that exists everywhere and every time is. And I can't feel everything either. I guess that other people don't know that either. By who or what is the balloon on the boundary sustained? Someday, I will travel beyond the limit of the world. Maybe there is a god somewhere beyond the edge. However, nobody can know about this. I think it's so ridiculous.

13th May

A wide open world in the garden of Hampton Court Palace

마을 밖 솔즈베리 들판에서 만난 넓게 펼쳐진 세상
A wide open world in the garden of Sallsbury field outside the village

빵을 문 다람쥐와 다른 믿음

벗어날 수 있을까? 숭고한 세상을. 그 가장자리도 모른 채. 그저 나는 세상에서 겪은 매 장소들과 마음 속 매 찰나들 사이에 있음을 느낀다. 어디인가? 그 사이를 알아차리기는 어렵다. 공간과 시간 사이에서 내 믿음은 길을 잃었나 보다. 저기 있는 한 삶처럼. 나는 공원에 사는 작은 다람쥐라고 상상한다. 나와 다람쥐 사이에 무엇이 다른지 잘 모른다.

우거진 푸른 풀밭 위를 걸을 때, 나는 한 그루 나무처럼 하늘과 땅 사이에 혼자라고 느낀다. 멈추어 생각에 잠길 때 나무를 타는 다람쥐를 본다. 다람쥐는 눈 깜짝할 사이에 빵 한 조각을 입에 물고 숨기느라 내달린다. 어디론가 사라진 다람쥐는 다시 공원 풀밭 위에 모습을 드러낸다. 아무것도 입에 물고 있지 않다. 그 빵이 어디 있는지 아무도 모른다.

다람쥐처럼 나는 어떤 것을 위해 늘 해 오고 있다. 이것은 다람쥐 굴레처럼 끊임없이 되풀이하는 삶의 막힘이자 벽이다. 나는 세상에서 늘 어떤 것을 찾아 모으고 있다. 그러나 이 막힘이 어디에서 왔는지 아직 잘 모른다. 내가 다람쥐가 아님을 밝히기 위해서 나는 세상 속 막힘이라는 굴레를 진지하게 생각할 날이 필요하다. 그 벽을 넘어설 순간이 오기나 할까?

My belief different from a squirrel with some bread [9)]

Can I escape from the world? The world is sublime. It means that the boundary is unknown. I just feel that something is in-between every place that I have experienced in the world and every moment in my mind. But I can't be conscious of something in between them. Where is it? Maybe my belief in between them like the maze of the world has disappeared. Like a life over there. Sometimes I imagine that I am like a bit of a squirrel's being that lives in the park near my home. I am not sure what the critical point of the difference between the two is.

As I am walking on the leafy green grass, I, like a tree, feel that I am alone in between the sky and the land. As I am thinking about something, I see that a squirrel runs up and down a tree. The squirrel goes off to hide a chunk of bread in the park after biting it off as slick as nothing at all. As slick as

---

9) 앞 사진은 마을의 클레어몬트 공원에 있는 벌레들을 위한 집 (The photo in the previous page is the house for bugs living in Claremont Garden)

nothing at all, the squirrel that disappeared from my view again exposes its appearance on the grass of the park. There is nothing in the mouth of the squirrel. I don't know where the bread is. Maybe nobody knows. The squirrel will again be running to discover, get and collect something.

Like the squirrel, I have always been doing something. This routine is like the squirrel's bridle as an endlessly repetitive restriction or a wall of life. I have always been discovering, getting, and collecting something in the world. But, I still don't certainly know where the restriction I know comes from. To verify that I am not the squirrel, I need a tough day thinking about the world's bridle of rules. Will the moment come beyond the invisible wall in my life?

16th May

늘 무언가를 궁금해 하는 사람
Human wondering about something

늘 무언가로 바쁜 다람쥐 (다음 쪽)
A squirrel's appearance with something all the time (The next page)

말하기 어려운 분위기 도취

날카롭게 찬 날은 가고 부드럽게 따스한 날이 오고 있다. 햄프튼 코트 궁 뒤 찬 하늘은 구름 모양에 붉어지고 템즈 강가 여왕 산책로 풀밭은 별처럼 밝게 빛나고 있다. 강 물 갖에는 산들바람이 분다. 풀밭에 앉거나 선 사람들 얼굴도 붉게 물들고 있다. 그들은 붉은 색 포도술 잔을 들고 있다. 강가를 거닐 때 잔 부딪히는 소리가 들린다. 그 소리들 사이 산들바람 속 풀들 속삭임을 느낀다.

사람들 얼굴에는 많은 순간들이 있다. 나는 그 얼굴을 그림판이라고 여긴다. 문득 그들 말을 들은 후 그 뒤에 숨은 이야기들을 상상한다. 여기에서 저기까지 강가를 따라 거닐 때 그들이 보여주는 것을 느낀다. 짧은 시간 따뜻한 강가를 거닐며 시간과 공간 사이 안에 있는 어떤 바람을 느낀다.

얼마나 많이 시간이 지났는지 궁금하다. 잠시 머물 어떤 곳을 찾는다. 한 번 본 적 없는 어떤 사람들 옆 풀밭에 털썩 앉는다. 천천히 둘러 본 후 저기 멀리 바라본다. 그 붉은 하늘 앞에 있는 나무, 물, 사람들을 살핀다. 천천히 눈을 감고 마음을 넓게 연다. 많은 순간들 기억 뒤편에 숨은 이야기들을 떠올린다. 나도 모르게 붉은 하늘 저 너머로 간다.

여왕산책로 풀밭에서 바라본 햄프튼 코튼 위 해지기 전 풍경
A view before sundown above Hampton Court Palace from the Queen's Promenade

Euphoria in a hard-to-speak atmosphere

Sharply cold days have been going away, and smoothly, warm days are coming in front of me. The cold sky behind the Hampton Court is reddening to the shape of clouds, and the grass on riverside Thames, Queen's Promenade, is brightly shining like stars. It is breezing over the water skin of the river. The faces of people who sit or lie on the grass in the riverside are also reddening. They are holding their wine glasses with a red color. When I am walking along the riverside, I can hear the clinking of the glasses. Between the sounds, I feel the whisper of the grasses in the breeze.

In their faces, there are many moments. I regard their faces as the canvases for their experiences. After I accidentally overhear what they are saying. I imagine lovely stories hiding behind their looks. From here to there, as I slowly am walking along the riverside, I feel what they are showing. When I stroll a short time through the riverside's warm promenade, I think of the wish for something in-between time and space.

I wonder how much time has passed. I'm looking for somewhere to leave for a moment. I plop down on the grass beside some people who I've never even seen. After I slowly look around, I am gazing into the distance. I look around trees, water, and people in front of the red sky. I slowly close my eyes and widely open my mind. I recall the various stories hiding behind my memory of moments. I go there beyond the red sky despite myself.

20th May

People who enjoy the Thames on board

여왕산책로 풀밭에서 바라본 햄프트 코튼 위 해질녘 노을
Sunset above Hampton Court Palace from the Queen's Promenade

"도시는 사는 사람이 알 수 있는 것보다 더 많은 것을 가지고 있지. 좋은 도시는 상상력을 불러일으키는 미지 (未知)와 가능성의 세계를 만들거든."
"A city always contains more than any inhabitant can know, and a great city always makes the unknown and the possible spurs to the imagination." Rebecca Solnit, *Wanderlust: A History of Walking*, 2001.

여왕산 책로 풀밭에서 나돌이를 하는 사람들
People talking on the grass on the River Thames

둥글게 미소 짓는 낯설지만 가까운 이웃

몇 달째 집 가까이 난 작은 길을 따라 걷고 있다. 거닐며 나뭇가지 사이로 희미해지는 해를 느끼며. 길 살은 포근포근하게 어두워지고 있다. 기대었던 시계탑 모퉁이를 도니 한 가족처럼 보이는 아주머니와 작은 여자아이가 다가오고 있다. 그들은 나를 보려는 게 아니다. 마음과 달리 그들과 이야기를 나눈 적도 없다. 길을 거닐 때마다 그들을 가끔 보곤 한다. 오늘도 마찬가지이다. 이번에는 귀여운 강아지가 없을 뿐이다.

곁을 지나친다. 그들은 사랑스러운 강아지에 대해 이야기하는 것처럼 보인다. 그들 눈과 마주칠 찰나에 나도 모르게 그들 낯빛을 읽는다. 작은 미소가 그들 입술에 맴돌고 있다. 어색하게 빙긋이 웃는다. 그들이 며칠 전 나에게 보낸 웃음을 떠올린다.

길 따라 시간을 탈 때 우리라는 느낌 뭉치에 맞닿은 알림이 미소를 떠올린다. 나는 알 수 있다. 홀로 집 밖을 거닐 때 가까이 사는 많은 사람들과 맞닿음이 있다. 그들이 나를 모르는 것처럼 나도 마찬가지이다. 그러나 작은 미소 띤 그들 낯을 기억할 것이다. 그들은 작지만 따뜻한 느낌을 내게 보낸다. 어느새 그들은 나를 위한 낯설지만 가까운 존재이다.

마을 모퉁이에 서있는 시계탑과 카페
Clocktower and cafe standing at the corner of the village

I have lived here for a few months and am walking alone along the small street between several houses near my home. While I stroll the road, I feel that the sun is glimmering in between the branches of street trees, and the atmosphere in the street is comfortably growing darker. When I turned the corner of the clock tower, one of the Surbiton attractions, I found that a lady and a little girl who look like a family were coming towards me. I quickly become aware that they are not coming to see me. Unlike my heart, I have never talked to them before. But whenever I stroll the street, I often have seen them. It is the same today. This time, there is no cute puppy with them.

I am passing them by. They seem to be talking about a lovely dog. As I contact their eyes at the moment, I am reading their facial expression despite myself. A small smile is touching their lips. I awkwardly give them my small smile too. I recall their smiles that they gave at me a few days ago.

When I ride a short time through the street, I recall the contact signals of their smiles for our emotional bonding. While I had been strolling around the outside of my home alone, I can cognize that there were many contacts with people who live near my home before I knew it. I don't know about them like they don't know about me. But I will remember their facial expression with small smiles. They convey little but warm sense to me. In no time, they are strange but familiar beings for me.

23rd May

킹스턴 광장에서 만나는 이웃들
Neighbors Meet at Kingston Square

마을 곳곳에서 만나는 낯선 사람들
Strangers who meet in every corner of town

마음 속 끊임없이 열리고 닫히는 창문

참 야릇하다. 약 백 년 전 노동자가 살던 집에 이리 살고 있으니. 많이 달라졌겠지만 그대로도 있으리라. 숨과 빛의 문, 창! 그 집 벽에는 갖가지 창이 있다. 나는 창으로 바깥을 보곤 한다. 이름 모를 재주꾼이 만든 여러 창들은 거의 네모 모양. 앞집 옆집 모두가 비슷하다. 창문은 중력을 헤아려 위아래로 여닫는다. 방 쓸모에 따라 창 위치가 다르다. 부엌과 거실 벽에 뚫린 앞창으로 집, 차, 나무, 길, 사람들을 본다. 침실과 공부방 벽에 난 뒤창으로는 뜰 잔디와 나뭇잎을 본다. 굽은 계단 옆창으로는 어렴풋이 하늘을 본다.

창이 세상의 눈이 듯 마음은 상상할 수 있는 세상의 창이다. 창은 나와 세상 사이에 있는 망원경 혹은 현미경이다. 창에 비친 스스로를 볼 수도 있다. 창틀은 혼란한 세상을 보이는 것과 보이지 않는 실체로 나눈다. 창 주변을 움직일 때 더 많이 세상 밖을 보고 느낄 수 있다. 그럼에도 불구하고 여전히 창 틀 너머 보이지 않는 세상을 느낀다.

운 좋게도 창 없이 세상을 드러내거나 모습 지을 수 있다. 마음 속 무한한 창을 느낀다. 여기에는 집의 창처럼 중력을 거슬러야 열 수 있는 물

리적 가장자리가 없다. 마음 속 창은 세상을 여기에서 저기로 지금부터 그 때로 넓힌다. 창을 통해 본 세상의 모습은 끝없나 보다. 눈을 감을 때마다 마음 속 보이지 않는 창을 연다. 끝없이 달려보려 하지만 어느 순간, 칠흙 같은 바다 속에서 길을 잃고 만다. 약 백 년 전에 이 집에 살았을 이름 모를 노동자 가족은 나와 같은 느낌이었을까? 식탁에 모여 앉아 밖을 들여다보는 그들의 방식에 빠져본다.

Endless opening and closing window in my mind

I feel strange. I can't believe I live in a house where a worker lived about a hundred years ago. Maybe it is a lot different from that in the past, but there are some things that have not changed. Windows as doors of air and light! There are various windows which are on each wall of my house. So, I can sometimes see the world through the windows. The frames of the windows made by an unknown craftsman are almost all rectangles with different shapes and patterns. All adjacent houses are similar. The windows are designed to open and close up and down, taking into account gravity. The windows vary in location depending on the use of the room. Through the front windows on the kitchen and living room in my house, I always see roads, houses, cars, trees, and people. Through the back window on the bedroom walls and study room walls, I often look at the grass in the yard and the leaves on the trees. Through the side window next to spiral stairs, I glimpse the sky from time to time.

As the windows are the eyes of the world, my mind has the imageable world's windows. I imagine that the window is a telescope or a microscope between the universe with the earth and me. Furthermore, I can see myself mirrored in the window. The frame of the window divides the chaotic world into visible and invisible reality. When I move around the window's space, I can see and feel the various outside world more than before. Nevertheless, I perceive that there is still the invisible world beyond the frame of the window.

Fortunately, I can represent or visualize the world without the windows. There are no physical restrictions here that can only be opened against gravity, like a house window. I perceive that there is an endless number of windows in my mind. The windows in my mind are augmenting my world from here to there and from now to then. I feel that my mind is surrounded by various windows. Maybe my windows are endless. Whenever I close my eyes, I open the invisible windows in my mind. I try to run endlessly, but at some moment, I get lost in the dark sea like a pitch black. Was it the same sense as me that the unnamed working-class family lived in this house about a hundred years ago? I fall into the way they sit at the table and look out.

30th May

보이지 않지만 창 밖 너머의 먼 풍경
Imaginary view beyond the window

창 밖에 보이는 뒤 뜰 나무
A backyard tree outside the window

하늘과 땅의 경계선 위에 떠있는 구름

오늘 리치먼드 공원에 있는 펨브로크 롯지 뒷마당에서 세상에 대한 건강한 질서를 느꼈던 백이십년 전 젊은 과학자, 버트런드 러셀처럼 막힘없는 하늘 너머 지평선을 느낀다. 지평선은 앞에 놓인 진짜 세상에 대한 모습을 두 조각으로 가른다. 그 모습 위쪽에는 하늘이 차지하고 아래쪽 반은 풀, 나무, 뾰족 지붕 등으로 찬다. 뭉게구름은 자연물과 인공물 윤곽을 특징짓는 두 부분 사이에 있는 지평선 너머에 흐리게 떠 있다.

두 팔을 펼쳤을 때 구름은 수평선 너머 내 품으로 오는 것처럼 보인다. 그 모습을 잡으려 할 때, 구름은 다른 세계에 떠있는 듯 궁금심을 일깨운다. 구름이 무엇을 닮았는지 생각하는 동안 감정이 얽힌 상상력이 불려온다. 구름 뒤에 다양한 척도들이 있다고 상상한다. 어릴 적 나는 구름이 솜사탕 같다고 생각 했었다. 상상력이라는 색채 팔레트로 그려진 구름 모양은 현실을 자극한다. 하늘을 배경으로 꿈틀거리는 구름의 윤곽선은 드넓은 우주 속으로 내 상상력을 데려간다.

상상하는 어떤 것은 지평선 위 구름 안에 있는 것 같다. 지평선 너머 갈 수는 있지만 그 상상하는 구름을 손으로 잡을 수 없으리라. 단지 구름으로부터 쏟아지는 끊임없는 이야기들을 느낀다. 아직 오지 않은 미래는 모르지만, 내 마음이 거기로 향하고 있다는 것을 알아차린다. 아마도 지평선 너머 사랑스러운 구름을 바라볼수록 나는 더 상상하게 될 게다. 이제 하늘로 달려가 지평선을 발판삼아 뛰어 올라 구름을 잡아 보련다.

Clouds floating above the boundary between the sky & the earth

I feel my horizon beyond an unimpeded view of the sky today like Bertrand Russel, a young scientist, felt the sound order of something in the world at the Pembroke Lodge's backyard in Richmond Park 120 years ago. The natural horizon divides a scene of the world that lies before me into two parts. The sky occupies the upward half of the view, and the downward half is packed with grass, trees, pitched roofs, and so on. Fluffy white clouds fascinatingly float over the horizon between the two parts characterizing it on the outline of natural objects and artifacts.

When I spread my arms, the clouds seem to be coming to my arms over the horizon. When I am captivated by the scenery, the clouds get me curious, as though I float in another world. They evoke my emotional imagination as I am thinking about what they look like. I imagine that there are various dimensions behind the clouds. As a kid, I used to infer the clouds as cotton candy and pretended the eat them. The shapes of the clouds painted with the color palette of imagination stimulate the reality around this place. The outline of the clouds wriggling in front of it against the sky takes my imagination to a vast universe.

The imaginary something is likely to be in the clouds over the horizon. Although I can go there beyond the horizon, I know that I can't catch the cloud's imaginary layers with my hands. I just feel that endless stories come pouring out from the shadows. Although I don't know the future to come to me, I perceive that my mind is toward there at this time. Maybe the more I look up at the lovely clouds over the horizon, the more I will become a dreamer. Now, I want to run to the sky and jump into the clouds with the horizon as a springboard.

5th June

Beautiful Tree Standing in Richmond Park

러셀처럼 뒷 마당에서 바라본 세상
My world from the back yard like B. Russell

땅 빛이 희미해지는 하얀 밤 열시

낮이 점점 길어질수록 기억할 수 있는 테두리는 점점 넓어지고 있다. 저녁을 먹은 후, 어두워질 때까지 나는 별 일 없이 밖으로 나가 산책하고 있다. 때론 나는 햄프튼 정원 위에 붉어진 하늘과 다채로운 구름을 보곤 한다. 그리고 이 곳 저 곳을 돌아다니면서 특별한 들풀, 사랑스러운 다람쥐, 애처로운 하루살이, 깊게 울리는 종처럼 동네에 의미를 주는 존재들과 만나는 걸 즐기고 있다.

세상에 어둠과 밝음 가장자리를 어떻게 알아차릴 수 있을까? 아마 그 자리가 있다면, 지금 내게 마주한 이 가장자리 시간이 바로 그 순간일 것 같다. 하늘이 어두워지는 동안 타는 듯 땅 빛은 희미해지고 있다. 교회 꼭대기에 매달린 종이 울릴 때에 서비튼에 내린 공허함은 성스러운 종소리 물결로 가득 찬다. 마음 떨림은 종소리 물결 따라 춤을 추고 있다.

고요한 어둠 속 지붕, 굴뚝, 나뭇가지 등 윤곽선이 흐릿해지고 가물거린다. 오묘한 존재들에 결부한 마음은 어두운 유리창에 비친 무표정함을 드러낸다. 이리저리 쪼개진 존재들은 사라지고 존재들 사이 감성 묶음은 거울처럼 유리창에 나타난다. 이름 없는 나뭇잎이 창문너머 바람에 펄럭이고 있다.

예술 건축물 같은 큰 슈퍼마켓. '기다려 장미'
A big supermarket like an art architecture. 'Waitrose'

10 o'clock at white night when the ground light fades

As the daytime is getting longer, the memorable scope is getting wider. After dinner, I usually go outside of my house and stroll the neighborhood until dark, without a particular purpose. Sometimes I used to see the reddening sky and the colorful cloud above the Hampton Court far away. And while I have wandered from place to place, I have been enjoying meeting with the beings that grant meaning to my neighborhood, like the particular weeds, the lovely squirrels, the pathetic dayflies, the soundly ringing bell, and so on.

How can I perceive the border between the edge of darkness and the edge of brightness in the world? Perhaps if there is a border, now this edge of time confronting me will seem to be just this moment. While the sky is getting darker, the glow of the land is getting dim. As the bell hanging at the top of the church ring, the emptiness around Surbiton is filled with the sacred sound wave. The pounding vibration in my heart is dancing along the waves of bell sound.

The reality's outline of roofs, chimneys, tree branches, etc., in calm darkness, is blurring and wavering. My heart, coupled with the mysterious beings, reveals an expressionlessness reflected on a dark glass pane. The complicatedly split beings disappear, and the being's emotional bonding appears on the scene on the glass as a mirror. The unnamed leaves are fluttering in the wind over the window.

13th June

HOBBS
LONDON

하얀 밤, 10시의 마을 모습
White Night, 10 o'clock in Surbiton

무엇인가 알기 어려운 비밀을 감춘 도시 바닥

'빅뱅' 이후, 인간 아닌 존재들을 아우르는 이름 없는 생물과 무생물의 활동 자국들을 쌓은 혼돈체인 도시 세계에는 불가사의한 바닥에 의해 이루어진 어떤 분위기가 있다. 서비튼에는 지구와 발 사이 표면인 도시 바닥이 있다. 땅, 바위, 잔디, 숲, 물 등으로 이루어진 이 바닥 형태와 특성은 긴 시간동안 우주 질서에 의해 영향을 받아 왔을 것이다.

루소가 말했던가? '도시는 인간 종이 만든 깊은 구렁텅이이다.' 서비튼에 있는 포장된 바닥 아래 거칠게 숨 쉬는 지구 표면을 본다. 나는 이 자연 바닥이 언제 덮였는지 모른다. 거꾸로 그 만큼 도시 상상력은 더 자라나는 듯하다. 그 바닥 아래 숨은 것과 그 위 드러난 것에 대해 기발한 궁금증이 솟아난다. 그 위를 걷자면 나는 장소 실마리들과 느슨한 분위기 뒤의 궁금증 조각들이 이어진 곳을 어렴풋이 알아차린다.

도시 표면을 덮은 이후 발자국들은 사라졌다. 만약 도시 바닥이 망가지지 않았다면 바닥 표면은 아마도 사람, 개, 고양이, 비둘기, 다람쥐, 여우 등 사냥꾼이 지난 발자국들로 가득 찼을지 모른다. 비록 그것을 보지 못하지만 발자국을 통해 짐작할 수 있다. 비록 어떤 것도 볼 수 없었겠지만 발자국의 모양과 크기에 의해 그것이 누구 것인지를 짐작할 수 있다. 언제부터인지 모르지만, 나는 서비튼에서 도시 바닥을 둘러보며 이 상상 그림을 그리는 중이다. 도시 곳곳에 있는 보이지 않는 발자국들은 나에게 몸 이동의 자유로움과 생각의 지평을 넓게 돕는다. 길 고양이처럼 그리고 레베카 솔닛이 말한 것처럼. '언어가 말할 수 있는 것을 막듯, 건축은 걸을 수 있는 곳을 막지만 걷는 사람은 다른 길을 찾아 낸다.' 고양이 발걸음처럼.

Urban floor hiding something like an obscure secret

There is an ambiance created by the mysterious 'floor' in the urban world which I call a chaotic reality through accumulated traces of anonymous activities in organic and inorganic entities, including non-human beings, after the Big Bang theorized by Dr. Hawking. There are 'urban floors,' which I call the surface between the earth and my feet in Surbiton. I infer that the form and character of the urban floors composed of soil, rocks, grasses, forests, water, and so on have been affected by the universe order for a long time.

Did Jean-Jacques Rousseau say, 'Cities are the abyss of the human species.' I regard the surface of the earth just breathing raggedly under urban floors paved in Surbiton. I do not know when the natural floors were artificially paved; to that extent, the urban imagination seems to grow paradoxically. It raises the whimsical questions of what is hidden under the urban floor and what is revealed on the urban floor. I am getting an inkling that the clues of places in Surbiton intend to connect with the pieces of curiosity from behind the relaxed and unconstrained ambiance as I walk on the urban floors.

After paving the earth's surface, it is obvious that footprints in an urban sphere like Surbiton have disappeared. If urban floors had remained untouched, the surface of urban floors would probably be full of footprints of the urban hunters like people, dogs, cats, doves, squirrels, foxes, etc. Even if I do not see them, I will be able to guess it through the footprints. Even if I did not see anyone, by the shape and size of the footprints, I would be able to guess whose it is. From time unknown, I am drawing an imaginary picture in this context while I look around on urban floors in Surbiton. The invisible footprints around the city world are helping me to broaden the horizon of my body movement and my thoughts. Like a street cat and like Rebecca Solnit said. 'Just as language limits what can be said, architecture limits where one can walk, but the walker invents other ways to go.' Like a cat's footsteps.

18th June

판판한 도시 바닥
-Flat urban floors

87

고르게 울퉁불퉁한 도시 바닥
Evenly bumpy urban floor

여러 가지가 모인 도시 바닥
Many things on urban floor

시간의 겹으로 온통 둘러싸인 광장

이 세상에 시간이 참으로 있을까? 공간처럼. 보거나 만질 수 있는가? 잇따르는 궁금증들. 여기에서도 마찬가지이다. 템즈 강을 따라 거닐 때마다 여왕산책로 끄트머리에 있는 다리를 본다. 템즈 강을 가르는 이 다리는 다가 갈수록 더 뜻있고 야릇하다. 오랜 중세부터 현재까지 이 중심지 안과 밖 사람들은 여기로 오고 갔을 게다. 다리 가까이 작은 공원, 카페, 음식점, 집 등이 옹기종기 붙어있다. 다리 밑에는 걷는 길, 배 정거장, 백조 쉼터 등이 함께 있다. 다리는 광장이 있는 좁은 길과 이어진다.

말 없는 다리를 뒤로 하고, 여왕 산책로에 이어진 좁은 옛 골목을 통해 광장 옆 가까이 다가간다. 건물 벽에 써놓은 역사 이야기를 살펴보니 이 광장은 중세시대 왕 즉위식이 있었던 상징성 있는 곳이란다. 골목 끝에 이르면 광장에서 벌어지는 여러 활동들을 볼 수 있는 순간이 찾아온다. 자유롭고 평화로운 활동들이 마음속으로 들어온다. 의자에 햇볕을 쬐는 사람들, 물 뿜는 분수에서 노는 어린이들, 입맞춤 하는 연인, 과일 매점에서 외치는 상인들, 식탁 옆 쉬고 있는 가족들, 무엇인가 이야기를 나누는 사람들, 아무 생각 없이 서있는 사람들 등이 있다.

햇빛은 살짝 기운 광장 바닥에 반사된 표면 위에서 습기와 함께 반짝이고 있다. 주변을 살펴보면 광장은 다섯 개가 넘는 길과 연결된다. 킹스턴 성격은 역사를 쌓은 다섯 개 길을 통해서 확장되고 길 바탕에 엮인 것처럼 보인다. 다채로운 활기는 이 길들과 이어진 광장에 매달려 있다. 오늘도 하늘에는 뭉게구름이 춤을 춘다.

킹스턴 다리와 주변 지역
Surrounding area of Kingston bridge

템즈강

특성지구
Area of Spcial Characte

기차역사

여객선터미널

사무실

문화시설

수택

다리

보행자권역

중소형상가

교회

보촌
Conserva

광장

햄튼코트

호그스밀강

수변산책로

관공서

뱃길

대학교

킹스턴 중심가 지도
Map of Kingston Centre

등록건물 (Listed Building)
지역등록건물 (Locally Listec
기념물 (Scheduled Monenm

Source: Sangphil. Park(2019), Implication of urban regeneration experiences in Lonon central areas, BDI

4
70M

Square surrounded by layers of time

Is there a true time in this world? Like space. Can I see or touch it? A series of questions. So are them here. While I walk along the Thames from my home to the Kingston area, I can see a structure called the Kingston Bridge laid over the river. Whenever I walk this path called the Queen's Promenade, I stare at the bridge located at the end of the path. The more I approach the bridge, the more meaningful and mysterious it is likely to appear. From medieval to present time, locals and outsiders of the Kingston area probably have come and went to communicate with each other through this bridge. Around the bridge are small parks, cafes, restaurants, and houses, and under the bridge are pedestrian roads, boat stations, and swan shelters. The bridge is connected to the center area of Kingston with its square.

With my silent legs behind me, I approach the square's side

through a narrow old alley that leads to the Queen's Promenade. I approach a side of the square. Through the historical story exhibits written on the building walls, I know that this square was a symbolic place where the medieval king was crowned. When I arrive at the end of the alley, I have a moment to catch sight of the people's activities in the square. Freely and peaceful activities are entering into my mind through my senses. I sense that many people are sunbathers on benches, children playing in the spouting fountain, a lovely couple kissing, merchants shouting in fruit stands, families resting by tables, people talking about something, people standing without thinking, and so on.

The sunshine is glittering with moisture on the reflecting surface of the urban floor of the slight tilting square. After looking around the square, I have noticed that the square is connected to over five paths. The Kingston area's character seems to be extended through the five paths accumulating history and being weaved based on these five paths. The different varieties of vitality are hanging over the square connected to the five paths. Today, the clouds of the sky are dancing in constant motion.

20th June

Model of Kingston centre in the Middle Ages

Source: Sangphil, Park(2019), Implication of urban regeneration experiences in Lonon central areas, BDI

떠난 누군가의 사랑스러운 이야기를 머금은 검은 의자

검게 칠해진 의자는 서비튼 곳곳에 있다. 주로 열린 공간 안. 의자 겉모습은 서로 닮았지만 놓인 환경에 따라 느낌이 다르다. 클레어몬트 공원 안에 식탁, 빅토리아 거리에 보는 갤러리, 서비튼 전쟁기념공원 옆에 뒤돌아 보는 공간, 서비튼 도서관의 상쾌한 정자, 여왕산책로의 감상하는 극장이라고 상상한다.

가지각색 의자들 사이에 잊을 수 없는 장소가 하나 있다. 감동스러운 메시지는 한 의자 등에 붙은 동판에 새겨 있다. '사랑하는 레마벤 모한랄 마네크포리아에 대한 기억 속에 (1937년 4월 2일 ~ 2016년 2월 21일). 나의 소중한 아내, 아름다운 어머니 그리고 훌륭한 나니마. 그리운 당신 미소, 마음에 새긴 기억. 당신은 우리 마음 안에 살고 우리 곁에서 걸으며 항상 우리를 안내해요.' 아마도 이 글은 그녀를 사랑하는 남편에 의해 쓰여진 것 같다. 이 의자는 그들이 이룬 사랑 이야기의 배경이다.

동네를 둘러 거닐 때 나는 이야기들을 새긴 의자들을 쉽게 발견할 수 있다. 의자에 홀로 앉아있는 동안 이야기 덕분에 외롭거나 지루하지 않다. 검정 나무의자들에 맺힌 공간 맥락 따라 이야기들이 흐른다. 서비튼에는 특별한 의자가 또 하나 있다. 의자가 있는 서비튼 전쟁기념공원은 1차 세계대전에서 죽은 이들을 기억하기 위한 장소이다. 그 의자에 앉을 때 나는 전쟁에서 목숨을 바친 용사들 이름을 새긴 비석을 볼 수 있다. 이 지역에 떨어진 수많은 폭탄들에 의해 부서진 집들의 조각들도 한 곳에 모여 있다. 이 의자는 아마도 많은 영혼들의 이야기를 담고 있을 게다. 따뜻한 산들바람이 풀 밭 위 비석들 사이에서 속삭인다.

서비튼 전쟁기념공원
Surbiton War Memorial

Black wooden bench with lovely stories

Black-painted benches are all over Surbiton, usually in open spaces. The benches resemble each other in their appearance but individualize their emotional images depending on circumstances. I imagine there are to be eating tables in Claremont Gardens, the seeing gallery by Victoria Street, the reflecting rooms near Surbiton War Memorial Ceremony, the refreshing gazebos by Surbiton Library, appreciating theatre along Queen' Promenade. There is an impressive and unforgettable place for me among the diverse benches.

A touching message is engraved on the copper plate stuck on the back of one of the benches. 'in loving memory of Remaben Mohanlal Manekporia (2nd April 1937 −21st February 2016). My dear wife, our beautiful Mummy, and wonderful Nanima. Your smile we miss, your memory we treasure. You live in our hearts and walk by our side, always our guide.' I guess that this message was probably written by her loving husband. The bench provides a backdrop for the story of their love.

As I walk around my neighborhood, I can easily find the benches embedding the stories. While I sit alone on the bench, I feel that I am not lonely or boring thanks to the story. The local stories flow along the spatial contexts involved around the black wooden benches in Surbiton. There is one bench in Surbiton that I think is the most special. The Surbiton War Memorial Ceremony Park, where the bench is located, is a place for remembering people who died during the 1st World War. When I sit on the bench, I can see the monuments bearing the names of warriors who have sacrificed their lives in the war and the fragments of houses destroyed by the numerous bombs falling into this area. This bench is probably involved in stories of many souls. A warm breeze is whispering among the monuments on the grass.

24th June

빅토리아 거리에 있는 검은 의자
A black chair on Victoria Street

"시골 풍경들은 영원(永遠)하고 새로 태어난 것 같은 이
중 환상을 줄 수 있지. 근데 도시는 특정 날짜의 건축물
로 표시되지. 사라진지 오래인 사람들이 지은 이 건축물
은 소라게처럼 우리가 기어오르는 껍질일 뿐이야.
"Rural landscapes can give the double illusion of
being eternal and newly born. Cities, on the
other hand, are marked with specific architecture
from specific dates, and this architecture, built
by long-vanished others for their own uses, is the
shell that we, like hermit crabs, climb into." Teju
Cole, *Known and Strange Things: Essays*, 2016.

여왕산책로 위에 있는 검은 의자
A black chair on the Queen's promenade

수수께끼로 가득 찬 세상, 경관 읽기

무슨 까닭일까? 어릴 적 시골 마을 언덕 위에서 넋 놓고 바라보던 여름 철 미리 내 때문인지, 별빛이 부서져 내린 것처럼 빛나던 겨울철 함박눈 때 문인지, 봄빛 병원에서 별 빛처럼 눈부셨던 딸의 눈빛을 처음 마주한 날 덕 인지는 잘 모른다. 언제가 처음인지 모르지만 나는 줄곧 세상 속에서 '경관' 이라고 불리는 '모습으로 드러난 세상'에 마음을 기울이고 있다. 어느 곳에 서나 불현 듯 알아차리는 세상에 대한 낯선 느낌의 일렁거림을 경관 현상으 로 보아야 할까? 세상의 모두와 이어진 경관을 나는 켜, 결, 터, 얼로 얼기 설기 읽곤 한다. 결코 말로 드러낼 수 없는 '모습으로 드러난 세상'이 무엇 이고 어떻게 그것을 이야기할 수 있을까?

세상에 있는 모든 삶터는 오랜 시간 동안 많은 사람들에 의해 시간이 차례차례 쌓인 켜가 있다. 만약 내가 삶터 땅 모두를 자세하게 들여다본 다면 이 켜들을 알아차릴 수 있을지 모른다. 결은 켜에 의해 영향을 받은 땅 겉 껍질에 새겨진 길, 건물, 구조물 등이 이루는 맺음에 의해 모양 지 은 바탕의 무늬를 뜻한다. 공간을 경험할 때마다 하늘, 산, 공원, 나무, 구 조물, 건물, 길, 시설물 등과 같은 여러 요소들에 의해 둘러싸인 어떤 모습을 느낀다. 공간은 삶과 죽음에 결부된 일상생활에 깊게 이어져 있다. 삶은 긴 시간동안 되풀이되고 사는 곳은 사는 이의 노력으로 끊이지 않고 이어질 수 있다는 것은 뚜렷해 보인다.

나는 삶터에 '설명하기 어려운 어떤 느낌'이 있으리라 생각한다. 때때로 생활 속 크고 작은 활동들은 곳곳에 스며든 보이지 않는 어떤 느낌을 일으킨다. 나는 땅과 하늘의 사이 공간이 알아차림을 넘어선 신비로운 어떤 느낌으로 뒤덮여 있다고 헤아린다. 만약 주의 깊게 어떤 곳을 둘러본다면, 삶에 관련된 공간과 대상에 접촉하고 알아차려 보이지 않는 무언가를 느낄 수 있을지 모른다. 오늘 나는 수수께끼가 가득한 세상 속 경관을 어서 읽어 보고 싶은 충동에 또 빠져버렸다. 갓 글 뗀 어린 장난꾸러기처럼.

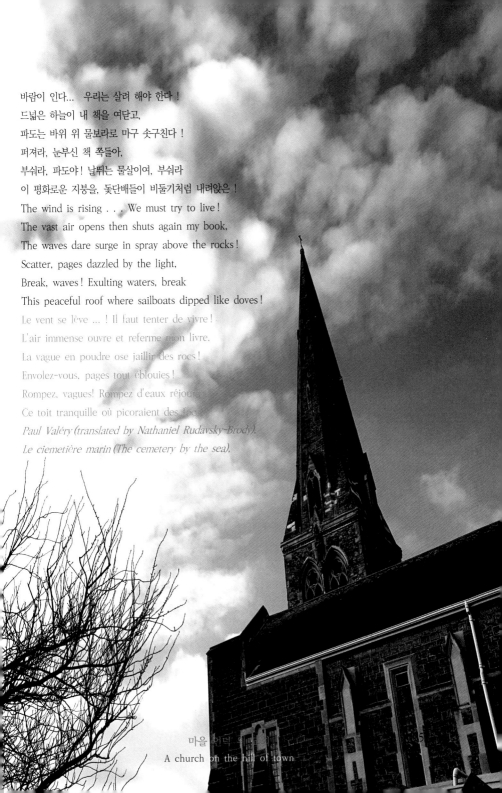

바람이 인다... 우리는 살려 해야 한다 !
드넓은 하늘이 내 책을 여닫고,
파도는 바위 위 물보라로 마구 솟구친다 !
퍼져라, 눈부신 책 쪽들아,
부숴라, 파도야 ! 날뛰는 물살이여, 부숴라
이 평화로운 지붕을, 돛단배들이 비둘기처럼 내려앉은 !
The wind is rising . . . We must try to live !
The vast air opens then shuts again my book,
The waves dare surge in spray above the rocks !
Scatter, pages dazzled by the light,
Break, waves ! Exulting waters, break
This peaceful roof where sailboats dipped like doves !
Le vent se lève ... ! Il faut tenter de vivre !
L'air immense ouvre et referme mon livre,
La vague en poudre ose jaillir des rocs !
Envolez-vous, pages tout éblouies !
Rompez, vagues ! Rompez d'eaux réjouie
Ce toit tranquille où picoraient des foc
Paul Valéry (translated by Nathaniel Rudavsky-Brody).
Le ciemetière marin (The cemetery by the sea).

마을 언덕 위의 교회

A church on the hill of town

Landscape reading on the world full of mystery

What is the reason? I don't know if it is because of the summer galaxy that I was looking at the rural neighborhood when I was a child, or because of the winter snow that shined like the starlight, or because of the first day I met my daughter's eyes that were dazzling like stars in a 'Bombit (Spring's light in English)' hospital. I do not know when it started, but I am concentrating on the world's landscape all the time. Should I regard the unfamiliar sensation that I suddenly perceive everywhere as the landscape phenomenon. I am trying to read the landscape connected to everything in the world using the four notions of time-accumulated layers ('Kyeo' in Korean), spatial textures ('Gyeol' in Korean), daily living places ('Teor' in Korean), and local atmosphere with soul ('Eol' in Korean). What is 'the world revealed by shape' that can never be revealed in words, and how can I understand and talk about it?

The human species have an amazing talent for configuring time. I feel certain that all settlements in the world have time-accumulated layers that have been gradually built up by many people over a long time. If I carefully excavate the land of all settlements, I will be able to find the time-accumulated layers. The spatial textures mean a living pattern formed by the relationship among streets, buildings, structures, etc., carved over the land surface affected by the time-accumulated layers. Whenever I experience space, I feel the scenery surrounded by diversified components; sky, mountains, parks, trees, structures, buildings, roads, street furniture, etc. The settlement is deeply connected to the daily life of people who are living in the living realm involved with life and death. It seems obvious that the life cycle of people is repetitive for a long time, and the existence can be infinitely sustained depending on people's efforts.

I think there is an 'unexplainable sense' in the living area, and sometimes the activities of the large and small life create an invisible sense that permeates the area. I imagine that the space

between the land and the sky is covered with a mysterious soul

beyond human perception and cognition. If I carefully look

around a local area, I may feel the invisible soul through

contacting and perceiving spaces and objects related to someone'

special life. Today I am again in the urge to read the landscape

in the world full of mystery quickly. Like a young naughty boy

who just learned to read.

23rd July

헴스테드 히스 언덕에서 바라본 런던의 모습
London view from the hill (Hampstead Heath)

WORKERS OF ALL LANDS
UNITE

MARX

Karl Marx tomb and giant monument in Highgate Cemetry

길 옆에 놓인 북적이는 붉은 빛깔 우체통

구름 사이로 내려온 빛이 속삭이는 걸까? 빅토리아 길을 두리번거리다가 자선 가게 앞 검은 빛 나무 의자에 앉는다. 보도 위 붉은 빛 철 상자. 그것은 검은 빛 쓰레기통 보다 크다. 앉아 있는 사이 나는 그 상자 안으로 흰 봉투를 조심스레 넣는 사람들을 보곤 한다. 봉투를 잡은 그들의 손. 하나로 모인 손가락 줄 맞춤. 알 수 없는 뜻 있는 이야기를 그 안에 넣었으리라. 누군가는 미소 짓고 다른 누군가는 시무룩한 낯이다.

빅토리아 길에 다다르기 위해 조금 내려간 뒤, 서비튼 역 앞 동그란 모양 교차로에서 오른쪽으로 돌면 많은 거리 시설물 가운데 붉은 우체통에 마주한다. 검은 색 나무 의자, 줄지은 나무들, 검은 빛 램프 기둥, 꽃바구니, 전기 상자, 검은 쓰레기통, 무감각한 포장 도로, 크고 작은 차양, 다채로운 상점 창문 등과 함께. 우체통은 마치 이야기가 가득한 나그네를 기다리는 것 같다.

거리를 거닐 때 나는 늘 그것을 만나고 가끔 곁에 머문다. 스스로 헤아린다. 이 상자에 누군가의 삶에 대한 여러 이야기가 가득 찼으리라. 손으로 직접 써내려간 글씨의 굵기와 모양은 그날의 느낌이 담긴다. 이런 맥락에서 우체통은 시민의 일상사를 담은 다큐멘터리 상자리라. 며칠 후, 이 이야기들은 봉투와 상자의 경계를 넘어 누군가의 마음으로 들어갈게다.

Red mailbox bustling on the side of roads

Was the light coming down through the clouds whispering to me? Being bewildered on Victoria street in Surbiton by something every time I sit on the black-wood bench in front of a charity shop, I usually see the red-colored iron box erected on the sidewalk. It is larger than the black-colored litter box also placed on the sidewalk. While I sit on the bench, I have often seen people who carefully put white envelopes into the iron box. At such time, I stared their hands grasping the envelope. Their fingers with side-by-side arrangement. I am sure that they probably have inserted meaningful stories that I am unable to know. Someone wears a smile, and someone else makes a long face.

To get to Victoria Street, I walk down one block, then turn

right at the roundabout in front of Surbiton station, and can easily find out the red postbox among the many street furniture; a black-colored bench, tree row, lamp poles with black colored skin, flower baskets, electric boxes, black litter bins, impassive pavement, big and small awnings, colorful shop windows and so on. I imagine the post boxes look like they are waiting for wanderers with stories riddled.

When I stroll on the streets of my neighborhood, I always meet them, and occasionally for a moment, I stand by them. About the boxes, I guess it is full of various stories, including a lot of messages about someone's life. The thickness and shape of the handwriting contain the sense of the day. I think that the postboxes can be regarded as documentary boxes filled with citizen's daily history. After a few days, the stories will spread beyond the envelope's boundaries and the box and be memorized by someone.

18th September

화려하게 치장한 머리와 같이 줄지은 꽃바구니

 빅토리아 길에 있는 꽃바구니 달린 등 기둥에 대해. 나는 매번 그 길 따라 있는 모자이크 바닥을 걸을 때마다 보도 위 검정 기둥에 달린 가지각색 바구니와 마주한다. 하나의 길 등에 두 꽃바구니가 매달린다. 그것들은 내 머리보다 크며 곱고 아름답다. 길을 걸을 때마다 나는 그 바구니 안에 있는 사랑스러운 꽃들을 얼핏 보는 사람들의 얼굴빛을 읽어보려 한다. 나는 꽃을 바라보는 그들 낯빛에서 어떤 표정이 드러나기를 바란다. 그 바구니를 매단 사람은 아마 내가 알 수 없는 어떤 뜻있는 이야기들을 담았을 게다. 무슨 뜻이 숨어있을까? 어떤 이는 웃고 어떤 이는 멍한 표정을 지은 채 걷는다.

 빅토리아 길에 다다르기에 앞서 한 블록을 걸어 내려가면 꽃바구니 없는 무표정한 나무와 잡초가 땅에 흩어진다. 서비튼 역 앞의 둥근 교차로에서 오른쪽으로 돌면 나는 마침내 많은 길 가구들과 사람들 사이에서 그 꽃바구니의 사랑스러운 줄지음에 마주한다. 나는 꽃바구니의 줄이 길 정원처럼 보인다고 상상한다. 그것은 내 머리 위에 다채로운 꽃들을 가진 작은 정원이다.

내가 마을의 사랑스러운 길을 걸을 때마다, 나는 항상 그 아름다움에 사로잡힌다. 내가 길 정원 같은 바구니 옆을 걸을 때, 나는 그것들이 누군가의 민감한 맞닿음에 이어진 다양한 감정들로 꽉 채워졌다고 헤아린다. 그 꽃바구니는 시민들의 일상적인 감정들로 가득 찬 정원이리라. 꽃바구니 줄을 훑어 본 후, 나는 바구니에 다양한 감정들이 채워져 누군가의 마음과 함께하리라 생각한다.

Flower basket lined up like gorgeously decorated hair

About the lamp pole with the flower baskets in Victoria Street. Every time I walk on the mosaic pavement along the street, I am faced with colorful baskets hanging on the black-colored lamp poles on the sidewalk. Two flower baskets hang on one streetlight. They are larger and brighter than my head. Whenever I walk on the street, I try to read the faces of people who catch a glimpse of the lovely flowers in the baskets. So, I expect to be revealed some expression in their faces which would like to look at the flowers. I am sure that the person who hangs it probably invested them with meaningful stories that I cannot know. What's the meaning behind them? Someone wears a smile, and someone else walks with a blank look on his or her face.

Before I arrive at Victoria Street, I walk down one block while I just see expressionless trees and wandering weeds on the ground without flower baskets. And then I turn right at the roundabout in front of Surbiton station and can finally find out the lovely rows of the flower baskets between people and the many street furniture. I imagine the rows of the flower baskets look like a street garden. It is a small garden with colorful flowers above my head.

Whenever I visit the lovely street in my neighborhood area, I am always captivated by the beauty. As I walk by the rows of baskets looking like a street garden, I guess they are full of various emotions, including many senses about someone's sensitive contacts. In this context, The flower baskets can be regarded as a garden of emotions filled with citizens' daily

sensations. After taking a glance at the rows, I figure to myself
that the various emotions will be filled into the baskets' space
and be shared with someone's mind.

19th September

해프톤 코트 궁 옆에 있는 장미 꽃 밭
Rose garden by Hampton Court Palace

가로등 꽃 바구니
A flower basket hanging from the waist of a streetlight

발을 대신해 바퀴로 돌아다니는 탈것

집 앞에 있을 때, 이리저리 길을 거닐 때, 그리고 도서관 갈 때, 친근한 바퀴를 단 크고 작은 탈것들과 마주하곤 한다. 붉은 빛깔 이층 버스, 지하철, 검정 택시, 자전거, 의자차, 유모차 등. 자세히 보면, 탈것이 가져야만 하는 길은 모든 나이와 성별을 지원하는 바퀴를 도와주게끔 만들어졌다. 그 길에 걸림을 찾을 수 없다. 길 겉은 부드럽고 판판하다.

얼마 전, 킹스턴 중심지에서 서비튼을 향한 칠십 일번 이층 버스를 탈 때다. 작은 바퀴를 단 의자차를 부리는 사람이 버스를 타려고 했다. 얼마 후, 내 걱정과 달리 큰 바퀴를 단 버스에 능숙하게 타는 의자 차에 앉은 그를 보았다. 버스와 길 사이의 틈은 넉넉히 좁다. 의자 차는 판판한 버스 바닥 위로 쉽게 오른다.

바퀴는 인류의 발이다. 오랫동안 바퀴는 인류의 발을 맡아 왔다. 버스는 이 마을에서 작은 탈것의 엄마차이다. 버스는 탈것을 여기에서 저기로 안전하고 안락하게 데려다 준다. 더 넓게 보면, 기차, 배, 비행기, 우주선은 인간 발 바퀴를 가진 작은 탈것을 엄마차에 옮기기 위한 이음매이다. 오늘 빅토리아 거리에서 잠시 변하지 않는 바퀴의 바탕으로써 사람들의 발을 본다. 세상에 서게 하는 발. 막힌 곳을 뚫는 발걸음. 앎을 향해 길을 닦는 발자국. 자유롭게 걸으니 이 어찌 기쁘지 아니한가?

Vehicle running around on a wheel instead of feet

When I have been in front of my house, when I have wandered from street to street in my neighborhood, and when I have headed Surbiton Library, I often find big and small vehicles with human-friendly wheels: red double-decker buses, tube trains, black cabs, bicycles, wheelchairs, baby carriages, and so on. Looking closer, I notice that the paths each vehicle has to take sincerely are made to assist wheels that support all ages and both genders. It is impossible to find any obstacles on the paths. All surfaces are smooth and flat.

A few days ago, as I was getting on the red double-decker bus, the number 71, at the central area of Kingston-Upon-Thames to Surbiton, I found that some people driving their vehicles with small wheels, baby carriages, and wheelchairs were trying to get on the bus at a stop. After a moment, contrary to my expectation, I saw that they, who are on vehicles with small wheels, were adept at getting on the bus, which is a vehicle with big wheels. The gap between the bus and the pavement is suitably narrow enough. I also noticed that people waiting with vehicles with small wheels were getting on the flat bottom of the bus easily.

I reckon the wheels of vehicles are feet of mankind. For a long time, the wheels of vehicles have substituted for the feet of mankind. A bus is 'a mother cab' of small vehicles in my neighborhood because a bus safely and comfortably takes small vehicles from here to there. Thinking more broadly, train, ship, airplane, and spacecraft are 'connectors' for conveying various small vehicles based on feet-of-mankind wheels to 'mother cabs.' Today, on Victoria street, I stare at the feet of people for a moment as an unchangeable basis of wheels. The foot that makes me stand in this world. Footstep piercing the blockage. Footprints to the path for accumulation of human knowledge. How glad is it to walk freely on Earth?

25th September

Walks on the flat street

빅토리아 길 모습

세상과 사람 몸 사이에 있는 인터페이스, 꾸밈새

꾸며진 낯선 즐거움? 네로 카페에 있는 사이, 마을 공원에서 쉬는 사이, 여왕 산책길을 거니는 사이에 여러 몸 모양새를 본다. 크고 작은 몸키, 희고 검은 피부 빛, 찌고 마른 부피, 굽고 곧은 모양, 파란 빛과 갈빛 눈동자 등. 가까이 가면 사람들 꾸밈새가 몸 모양새에 따라 새삼스럽다. 못남은 찾기 어렵다. 저마다 아름다움이 다르기에. 몸 모양새 덕인지 꾸밈새 탓인지 모르지만.

얼마 전 서비튼 지역의 빅토리아 거리에 있는 카페 창 옆 소파에 앉아 걷는 이들을 보고 있었다. 천 맵시, 두드러진 액세서리 등으로 꾸민 사람들이 길거리와 카페에서 스스로를 뽐내고 있었다. 어쩌면 그렇게 보인건지도 모른다. 몸을 가린 꾸밈새와 거리 풍경의 어우러짐. 거리에서 사물과 사람의 갖 사이에 적절한 마음 졸임이 있다고 느낀다. 여러 꾸밈새를 갖춘 사람들이 거리를 우아하게 걷거나 열린 공간에 앉아 있는 사이에 어느 정도 거리를 두고 있다. 같은 극을 띤 자석처럼.

나는 사람들의 꾸밈새가 인류의 갖이라고 생각한다. 오랫동안 사람들의 꾸밈새가 인류의 갖을 맡아 왔다. 인류의 갖은 일상생활의 여러 맥락에서 조율된 경계면인 것 같다. 몸과 환경의 경계면이 여러 사물과 관계 맺기 때문이다. 더 넓게 보면 몸과 세상 사이의 모든 공간은 아마도 여러 갖으로 이루어진 경계면이리라. 오늘 나는 빅토리아 길에서 꾸밈새를 넘어선 상상의 현실로 사람들 주변의 경계면을 얼핏 살핀다. 자연스럽거나 억지스러운 여러 갖 꾸밈 세상 ! 자연과 인문 사이 경계는 틀림없이 어디일까 ?

여러 꾸밈새가 만나는 거리풍경
Streetscape with various embellishments

"도시는 시간을 재기 위해, 그리고 자연에서 시간을 없애기 위해 만들어졌지. 거기에는 끊임없이 세는 것이 있어."라고 그는 말했다. "네가 그 모든 갖을 벗겨 내고 그 안을 들여다보면 남는 것은 공포야. 문학이 치료하려는 것이지."

"Cities were built to measure time, to remove time from nature. There's an endless counting down, he said. When you strip away all the surfaces, when you see into it, what's left is terror. This is the thing that literature was meant to cure." Don DeLillo, *Point Omega*, 2010.

"내가 도시에 있을 때마다 폭동이 매일 일어나지 않는 게 의아하다. 대학살, 끔찍한 살육, 최후의 날 혼돈. 그렇게 많은 인간이 서로 미워하지도 않은 채 어떻게 그리 좁은 공간에 공존할 수 있을까?"

"Whenever I happen to be in a city of any size, I marvel that riots do not break out everyday: Massacres, unspeakable carnage, a doomsday chaos. How can so many human beings coexist in a space so confined without hating each other to death?" Emil Cioran, *History and Utopia*, 1987.

지구와 나를 연결하는 꾸밈새, 구름
Cloud, the ornament that connects the Earth and me

Embellishments between the world and the body

Strange pleasures decorated by something? While in the Cafe Nero, while resting in the village park, and while strolling around the Queen's Promenade along the River Thames, I often see people with various body features: tall and short height, white and black skin, fat and thin volume, bent and straight shape, blue and brown pupils and so on. When I open my eyes wide, I feel that the embellishment of people is varied with the characteristics of their bodies. It's hard to find ugly. Each has a beauty. I don't know if it's because of the body's features or the embellishments.

A few days ago, sitting on a sofa with a window view in a coffee shop by Victoria Street, Surbiton, and looking at people walking around the street, I found that some people wearing their fashions decorated with various items-fabric patterns, unique accessories and so on-were trying to show them off on the street and in the coffee shop. Maybe that's what it looked like. The embellishment of the body blending with the landscape of the street. I felt that there was adequate tension between the skin of objects and the people's flesh on the street. When people with different ornaments walked gracefully through the streets or sat in open spaces, they were at some distance. Like magnets with the same pole.

I reckon people's embellishment is the skin of mankind. For a long time, they have substituted for the skin of mankind. The flesh of mankind seems to be an interface coordinated in various contexts in daily life because the interface between body and environment interacts with multiple objects in the street. Thinking more broadly, all spaces between the body and the world is probably composed of multi-layered interfaces. Today, by Victoria Street, I look at the interface around people for a moment as an imaginative reality beyond embellishment. About the multi-layered world concerning natural or forcible embellishments! Where is the boundary between nature and humanities exactly?

25th September

인공 꾸밈새의 광장 풍경
Squarescape of artificial ornaments

내 마음을 맴도는 비오는 추수 축제

이슬비 내리는 날. 아직 런던이 어리둥절하고 옛 골목에 이어진 킹스턴 고대 광장의 성격을 잘 몰랐던 나는 여기에 사는 한국인이 여는 추수 축제 분위기가 궁금했다. 설레는 마음을 숨긴 채 쉬고 싶어 하는 아내와 딸을 겨우 달래어 집을 바삐 나섰다. 얼마나 지났을까? 축제 자리에 들어설 때 익숙한 멜로디 물결이 귓가에 맴돌았고, 은밀한 냄새가 코끝을 간지럽혔다. 구 시청 앞에 임시로 꾸민 무대에서 곱게 꾸민 젊은이들이 옷에 스며 든 빗방울을 잊고 즐겁게 춤을 추고 있었다. 봄철에 들렸던 이사벨라 농장의 꽃 풍경 같은 분위기라고나 할까 ?

광장에 다다르자마자 나는 1840년에 지어져 최근 다시 살린 구 시청사를 바로 알아보았다. 구백년 즈음 된 모든 성자들의 교회, 시장 광장, 주변 가게, 중세 거리 느낌으로 광장과 이어진 다섯 골목. 시간으로 꾸며진 광장 한가운데에 빽빽하게 모인 작은 하얀 가게 사이의 갈라진 공간에서 나는 촉촉한 눈으로 서있는 사람들과 지나가는 사람들 무리를 훑어보았다.

이곳에서 한국 추수 감사절 한가위의 의미는 무엇인가? 보름달에 관한 전설의 마법인가? 밑바닥 없는 목마름에서 하늘 없는 그리움에 이르기까

지, 내 가슴 속의 감정적인 날개 깃털은 힘이 넘치는 광장에서 나란히 펄

럭이고 있었다. 비오는 바로 그 날 다양한 물건과 다채로운 사람들이 섞

인 낯선 친숙함에 사로 잡혔다. 무대 위에서 흔들리는 어깨 너머로 비가

내리는 동안 나는 어색함 없이 유쾌함으로 깊은 어울림에 빠져 들었다.

비오는 추수축제에 빠져

The rainy Harvest Festival

The rainy Harvest Festival wandering my heart

It was a day it was drizzling. I, who was still bewildered in London identity and did not know well about Kingston Market Square's character, an ancient historic place connected to old alleys, wondered what the Harvest Festival hosted by Koreans who live in Kingston-Upon-Thames area what kind of ambiance will be. I kept my heart on the line and managed to persuade my wife and daughter to rest, to hurry out of the house. How long had it been? As soon as I entered the festival place, a wave of familiar melody hovered around my ears, and intimate smell movement tickled the end of my nose. On a temporally embellished stage in front of Old Town Hall, young, colorful people were dancing joyfully together as they forgot the drip of rain permeated into their clothes. The atmosphere like the Isabella Plantation that my family visited last spring comes to mind.

After I arrived at the square, I immediately distinguished the Old

Town Hall built in 1840 and recently restored. All Saints Church, which is about 900 years old, Market Square, the commercial buildings around the square, five alleys connected to the square in the Medieval street pattern. In the split space among white booths clustered in the centre of the time-adorned square, I looked through the throng of standing people and passers-by with moist eyes.

What is the meaning of Hangawi, Korean Thanksgiving Day, in London of UK? Is it magic of legend concerning the full moon? From bottomless thirst to skyless yearning, the emotional feathers of wings in my heart were fluttering side by side in the vibrant square. The very day on a rainy day, I was caught up in a strange familiarity mixed with various objects and colorful people. Looking over shoulders shaking on the stage while the rain was coming down, I sank into the deep spirit of togetherness with conviviality without awkwardness.

1st October

봄철에 꽃이 피는 아름다운 꽃 풍경
Spring flowerscape in Isabella Plantation

마을사람들의 행진과 함께 시작한 서비튼 마을 잔치

햇빛이 눈부신 날. 나는 여전히 런던 어딘가를 떠돌며 마을을 조금씩 알아가고 있다. 오늘은 마을 잔칫날이다. 얼마 전부터 마을 곳곳에 잔치를 알리는 포스터가 붙고 마을 홈페이지가 떠들썩했다. 매년 열리는 이 마을 잔치를 나는 한차례만 겪을 수 있기에 처음부터 꼭 함께 하고 싶었다. 아침밥을 서둘러 해치우고 집에서 나섰건만 벌써 사람들이 곳곳에서 웅성거렸다. 사람이 가장 많이 몰린 마을 교회 옆 앤드류 길에는 참전 용사, 자원 봉사자, 클래식 자동차, 말 탄 경찰 등이 줄지어 행진하고 있었다.

나는 길에 들어서서 이웃들과 함께 앤드류 길부터 빅토리아 길을 거쳐 클레어먼트 정원까지 그 행진을 따라갔다. 그 사이 나는 마음과 이어진 익숙해진 장소들을 아직 낯선 이웃들과 함께 차례로 만났다. 늘 보던 세인트 앤드류 교회, 가끔 한잔 하던 빅토리아와 서비튼 플라이어 펍, 중고 책을 사러 들리던 심장재단 자선가게, 지나던 서비튼역, 둥근 교차로, 몸을 기대던 뾰족 시계탑, 클레어먼트 정원. 그리고 왠지 마음 가는 고양이.

오늘 끝날 것 같지 않은 쓸쓸함부터 끝없는 활력까지 마음 속 순간의 감성 자국들은 길 따라 여기저기로 흩어졌다. 행진 뒤, 클레어먼트 정원에서 사람들과 함께 음악 공연, 야외 전시회, 임시 동물원 등으로 즐겁게 시간을 보냈다. 마신 맥주 탓인지 내리쬔 햇빛 탓인지 붉어진 얼굴빛을 하고 집으로 돌아왔다. 마을이 빛나던 바로 그날, 나는 친숙한 표현과 낯선 이웃이 섞인 무른 길듦에 사로 잡혔다. 길 위 뽐내는 다리들을 보면서, 햇살이 내리는 사이, 나는 기꺼이 큰 공동체의 느낌 거울에 비치고 있었다.

행진하는 이웃들
Marching neighbors

137

The Surbiton Festival started with the march of Surbitoners

A day when the sunlight was shining. I was still roving around London somewhere and getting a little bit of the character in the neighborhood. Today is the day of the Surbiton Festival, hosted by my neighbors. I have been informed about the festival since I have been posting festival posters all over the neighborhood, and the homepage of the neighborhood has been buzzing. I wanted to see this annual festival from the beginning because I could only experience it once. As soon as I had a quick breakfast and left the house, people were already buzzing around. Dozens of people march in St Andrews Road, including war veterans, older people, young volunteers, classic car drivers, and horse-riding police.

After I entered the road, I, together with many Surbitoners, attentively followed the parade from St. Andrews Road to Claremont Gardens via Victoria Road. While I was marching in the parade, I met in with familiar places linked with my heart one by one with my strange neighbors: the St. Andrews Church, which I always had seen, The Victoria and The Surbiton Flyer Pub which I occasionally had a beer, British Heart Foundation where I sometimes had bought secondhand books, the Surbiton Station which I had been used to pass through, the roundabout through which I had used to drive, the Clock Tower which surface I often had leaned against, the Claremont Gardens which I had sat in thoughtful silence. And the lovely street cat for some reason.

From horizonless dreariness to boundless vivacity, the vibrant mark of the moment in my heart was strewed from a spot to another along the walking road. After the march, I spent time with the Claremont Gardens' scattered people, enjoying music performances, outdoor exhibitions, and makeshift zoos. I went home with a reddish face, either because of the beer I drank around or because of the sunlight. The very day in the

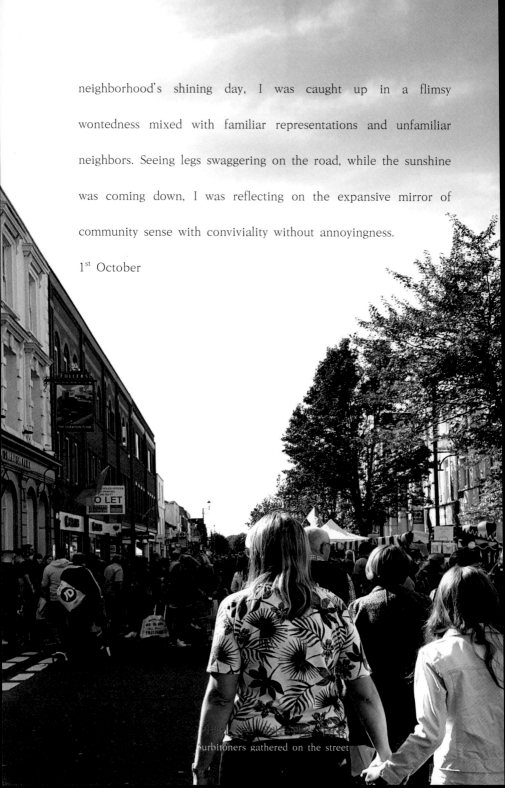

neighborhood's shining day, I was caught up in a flimsy wontedness mixed with familiar representations and unfamiliar neighbors. Seeing legs swaggering on the road, while the sunshine was coming down, I was reflecting on the expansive mirror of community sense with conviviality without annoyingness.

1st October

Surbitoners gathered on the street

Baby horse with sad eyes

이리저리 실험하는 햄프튼 코트 궁

궁은 왜 이리 크고 비비꼬인 모양일까? 오백년 전 즈음 헨리 8세 이야기가 이어진 곳. 크고 작은 공간은 병치하면서 서로 엮인다. 햄프튼 코트 궁 안쪽은 왕 집, 미로 방, 복도 그물, 여러 모양과 크기를 가진 안뜰이 나란히 놓이고 벽이 마주한다. 이쪽에서 저쪽으로 가려면 벽 사이 장소 묶음과 만난다. 궁 안쪽에 작게 나뉜 장소들은 곧은길에 이어지지 않고 미로 그물로 얽혀 있기에 계속 골라야 하는 길에 빠지고 만다. 많은 고르기를 하면서 나는 내가 어디에 있고 어디로 가는지 모르는 걸 알게 된다. 그때 비로소 나 스스로를 되돌아 볼 순간과 마주한다.

거꾸로 궁의 바깥 공간은 왕 정원, 퍼즐 잔디밭, 대칭 자갈길, 상징 분수 위치 및 나무 배열이 마주하면서 을러댄다. 여기에서 저기로 움직이려면 버섯 모양의 나무 사이 공간에서 마음이 내리눌린다. 여러 개로 나뉜 장소는 절묘한 정원이 아니라 직선 및 원형 경로 체계와 서로 이어지기에 또렷한 시각적 길을 가진 투시도에 빠진다. 고를 여지 없이 나는 내가 어디에 있고 어디로 가는지 알고 있다는 것을 알게 된다. 그 때 비로소 나 자신의 외로움을 볼 고르기의 순간이 있다.

142

성벽 안팎으로 많은 사람들이 왕궁에서 살았었다. 많은 역사적 순간이 궁 공간 사이에 혼란스러운 감을 가지고 있지만 그 이야기는 사람들의 마음에 남아 있다. 왕의 이야기를 넘어서 궁 안쪽 공간의 뜰에 있는 포도주 분수대 옆에 털썩 앉는다. 먼 옛날에 목을 축이던 지친 농민들이 내 옆에 있는 듯하다. 풀려서 비비꼬인 발걸음으로 왕궁을 빠져 나왔다. 템즈 강을 따라 걸으며 멀리서 강을 흐르는 작은 배를 바라본다. 힘차게 노 젓는 사람들의 모습이 오늘따라 더 즐거워 보인다.

The wine fountain inside Hampton Court Palace

Why is the palace big in size and entangled in form? This is a unique place that linked with the story of Henry VIII about five hundred years ago. The shape and size of the space are interwoven together while juxtaposing. In Hampton Court Palace's indoor space, the king's house, a maze of rooms, a network of corridors, a juxtaposition of courtyards in various shapes and sizes, and an arrangement of walls face and weave together. To move from one place to another, I always have a choice in a bundle of places in-between walls: because ramified places in indoor space of the palace are not connected to a straight path system but are interlaced with a tangled web, I am so confused by an endless path of choice. After having many options, I become aware that I do not know where I am and where I go. Then and not till then, I have a moment of choice to look back at myself.

On the contrary, in the palace's main outdoor space, a garden of kings, a simple puzzle of grass plots, asymmetry of gravel paths, a symbolic position of a fountain, and an arrangement of trees face away and align imposingly. To move from here to there, I always have a pressure in the space among toadstool-shaped trees: because the places subdivided in the outdoor area of the palace are not composed of an exquisite garden but interrelated to both straight and round path system, I cannot help but fall into a perspective view with simply optical routes. After having little choice, I become aware that I know where I am and where I go. Then and not till then, I have a moment of choice to look at my won loneliness.

Inside and outside walls and plots, many people lived in the king's palace for a long time. Although many historical moments have chaotic senses between object and space in the castle, clues of his and her stories remain in people's minds. Beyond the king's story, I sit down next to the wine fountain on the base court in the palace, and I feel as if the weary peasants who have been thirsty in the past are next to me. I slipped out of the castle with a twisted step. Walking along the Thames, I look at the small boat flowing along the river from a distance. People rowing vigorously seem more enjoyable today.

13th October

Around Hampton Court Palace building

A straight figure outside Hampton Court Palace

집 딸린 정원, 정원 딸린 집

이 마을에는 왜 이렇게 법원이 많지? 아니면 궁궐인가? 테니스 경기장일지도 모른다. 놀랍게도 그것은 조금 큰 집일 뿐이다. 이 동네에는 무동, 파이퍼스, 판도라, 에바시 등 사람들이 사는 집 딸린 정원이 많이 있다. 거주자 아파트인 집 딸린 정원의 실내 공간에는 한 묶음의 방, 공용 복도, 베란다 및 벽이 서로 마주보고 줄짓는다. 한 장소에서 다른 장소로 움직이려면 벽 사이에서 여러 장소를 고를 수 없다. 집 안쪽 공간에 있는 장소가 한 길로 연결되어 있기에 차례로 움직일 수 있다. 고른 뒤에는 내가 어디 있고 어디로 가는지 쉽게 알 수 있다. 집에 다다르기에 앞서 뒤 돌아볼 틈을 주지 않는다.

마찬가지로 집 딸린 정원 바깥은 주민을 위한 정원, 수수한 잔디 배치, 대칭 포장, 상징 꽃 위치 및 나무가 서로 마주보고 줄짓는다. 자그마하고 아기자기하다. 자리를 이동하기 위해 햄프튼 코트 궁처럼 나무들 사이의 복잡한 공간에서 길을 어렵게 고를 필요가 없다. 집 딸린 정원의 바깥 공간은 절묘한 정원이 아닌 길 하나에 엮여 있기에 그 공간의 부분을 한 눈에 읽을 수 있다. 하나를 고르면 내가 어디 있고 어디로 가는지 알게 된다. 정원

집 입구에 다다르기 전, 나는 스스로를 돌아볼 틈이 없다.

벽과 장소 안팎에서 많은 사람들이 오랫동안 집 딸린 정원에서 살아 왔다. 많은 순간이 지나 갔지만 이 집 딸린 정원에서 사물과 공간 사이에 그들의 이야기가 남을 것이다. 사는 사람의 이야기를 넘어 집 딸린 정원의 바깥 공간 앞 정원에서 나는 나무 옆에 쉬는 많은 이야기를 가진 거주자들의 모습을 상상한다. 집 딸린 정원을 지나 길을 걷다 보면 함께 걷는 사람들이 느껴진다. 고양이가 나를 따뜻하게 맞이한다.

바깥 공간을 살피는 고양이
A Cat looking outside space

Garden with a house, house with a garden

Why are there so many courts in this neighborhood? Or a palace? It may be a tennis court. Surprisingly, it's just a little big house. In this neighborhood, there are many courts in which citizens live: Meudon, Pipers, Pandora, Embassy, etc. In a court's indoor space, an apartment of dwellers, a unitary set of rooms, a common corridor, an addition of a veranda, and an allocation of walls face and align each other. To move from one place to another, I do not choose a bundle of places in between walls: because places in the indoor space of the house are connected to a single path system, I can move in an order with a simple route. After choosing, I become aware that I easily know where I am and where I go. Before I arrive at a housing unit in a court, I have a moment of no choice to look back at myself.

Similarly, in the court's primary outdoor space, a garden for residents, a simple lawn layout, a symmetry of pavement, a symbolic position of flowers, and an arrangement of trees face, and align each other. It is petite and dainty. To move from here to there, like Hampton Court Palace, I don't have to make it challenging to choose a path in the complex space between trees. Because places in the outdoor area of a court are not composed of an exquisite garden but hung on a single path system, I can read parts of the space with optional views. After choosing a view, I become aware that I know where I am and where I go. Before I arrive at a court entrance, I do not have a moment of another choice to look back at myself.

In and out walls and places, many dwellers have lived in the courts for a long time. Although many personal moments have passed, senses embedded between objects and space in the court with memories of their stories will remain in their minds. Beyond the resident's stories, I imagine a scene of different kinds of dwellers with many stories resting by trees in the front garden of the court's outdoor space. After I pass by the court,

as I am walking along the road, I seem to hear the magical

voice of someone walking with me. The cat greets me warmly.

13th October

Flowers in a garden

집 밖 공간에 연결된 작은 마을 공원.
A small neighborhood park connected to the space outside the court

다시 자연으로 돌아간 시골 마을

시간은 익숙한 모습을 낯선 모습으로 되돌리는 마법을 가진 모양이다. 잉글랜드 서쪽 지역에 위치한 코츠 월드 지역의 시골 마을은 그림 같은 분위기가 있다. 솜구름이 있는 하늘과 푸른 들판이 있는 땅 사이의 풍경에 탐닉하는 동안 나는 종종 동화 같은 마을과 만난다. 자연 환경의 역사적인 마을을 지날 때 내 눈동자는 그 특징 앞에서 커진다. 물줄기와 언덕 경사면 사이에 쌓인 토착 유물, 오두막 사이의 생체형 골목, 자연 경사를 따라 비스듬한 지붕의 사랑스러운 반복, 오랫동안 깔끔하게 쌓인 벽돌로 된 벽의 놀라운 연속성, 나무틀이 있는 비슷비슷한 창문 등.

윌리엄 모리스(1834-96)가 '영국에서 가장 아름다운 마을'이라고 칭한 비버리 마을 골목길을 걷다 보면 추위에도 불구하고 편안하고 매혹적이다. 지역 분위기가 있는 그림 같은 모습은 드넓은 하늘 아래 산비탈에서 자라는 이름 없는 풀을 비롯한 나무와 함께, 사람들이 지나며 만든 골목과 이름 모를 목수가 지은 옛 오두막에 연결될 게다. 나는 촉촉한 흙과 조약돌이 내 발바닥을 통해 골목길의 갗에서 튀어 나오는 것을 느낀다.

담쟁이가 오두막 벽을 기어올라 덮고 있다. 담쟁이 줄기와 잎 사이에

154

있는 별장을 잠시 바라보자니 시간이 얼마나 흘렀는지 모르지만 벽돌이나 돌 갖을 통해 마을 역사의 자국을 발견한다. 이 시골 마을이 시간이 지남에 따라 점점 더 자연을 닮아 가고 있음을 안다. 비버리 마을은 자연의 일부가 된 것 같다. 마음 속에서 더 이상 자연에서 마을을 떼어 놓을 수 없다. 그것은 자연의 일부일 뿐이다.

여전히 사람이 살고 있는 옛 마을 풍경
An old village landscape still inhabited by people

시간이 묻은 집
A time-laden house

Country village back to nature

Time seems to have the magic of returning familiar scenes to strange scenes. There is an ambiance about the picturesqueness in the features of country villages in Cotswold District County, located in the western area of England. While I am indulging in the scenery between the sky with cotton clouds and the land with green fields, I often meet with fairy-tale villages. When I go by each historical village in the natural environment, the pupils of my eyes dilate before the features: vernacular artifacts built up between water stream and hillslope, biomorphic alleys among cottages, lovely repetition of sloping roofs along a natural slope, impressive continuity of walls with bricks piled up neatly over a long time, similar features of windows with wooden frames, etc.

When I walk along an alley in Bibury village, described by William Morris (1834-96) as 'the most beautiful village in

England,' I feel comfortable and charmed despite the bitterly cold chill. The picturesque scenery of the local atmosphere is likely connected to old cottages built by obscure carpenters and alleys formed by passing people, with nameless weeds and trees growing on the hillside below the wide sky. I sense moist soil and pebbles sticking out of the surface of the alley through the soles of my feet.

The ivy is creeping up a cottage wall and even covering it. When I stare at a cottage wall between the stems and leaves of the ivy for a while, although I don't know how much time passed, I find traces of the village's history through the surface of bricks or stones on the wall. In this country village, I grasp that the village takes after nature more and more each day. The Bibury village seems to become a part of nature. Even in my mind, I am no longer able to detach the village from nature. It is just a part of nature.

29th October

자연을 품은 건축물
A building resembling nature

자연의 한 부분이 된 옛 마을 풍경
A old village as a part of nature

시간 위에서 춤추는 박물관 같은 도시 중심지

서비튼에서 워털루까지 기차로 삼십분 즈음. 런던 중심에 있는 '스퀘어 마일'로 알려진 '시티 오브 런던' 지역은 넉넉한 분위기이다. 면 구름이 펼쳐진 하늘과 크고 작은 돌들이 뿌려진 땅 사이에 우아한 건물들 사이로 거닐다 보면 잔잔한 풍경을 통해 다양한 감각을 얻는다. 길을 거닐 때 나타나는 여러 특징들 앞에 눈동자는 넓어진다. 반듯한 큰 길과 구불구불한 좁은 골목 사이 긴장감, 건물이 이루는 다양한 길 벽, 역사적 장소와 높은 현대적 건물 사이의 병치 등이 있다. 공간 언어가 빚는 수수께끼!

'스퀘어 마일'에 있는 길에 머물 때 찬 공기에도 불구하고 깜짝 놀라고 설레는 느낌이 든다. 런던 역사에 관한 많은 유산이 이천년 넘게 삶 속에서 진화해 왔기 때문이다. 이 분위기의 독특한 느낌은 넓은 하늘 아래 건물과 가로 시설물이 있는 장소의 얼과 연결되어 있는 것 같다. 이 느낌에 덧붙여, 나는 발바닥 피부 세포에 전달되는 길의 자갈 갖을 통해 장소의 첫 모양을 느낀다. 시간을 느낌 짓는 도시 껍질, 갖!

건물 사이에 빈틈이 없기에 길 벽은 주로 건물 정면으로 이루어진다. 잠시 길 벽을 보면 여기 시간이 얼마나 흘렀는지 모르지만 나는 벽돌이나

돌 갗을 통해 길 이야기를 헤아려 본다. 이곳에서 나는 시간 흐름에 따라 중심지가 점점 더 역사박물관이 되어가는 상상에 마음을 사로 잡혔다. 이 '스퀘어 마일' 지역은 박물관의 일부인 것 같다. 마음속에서도 더 이상 런던 박물관에서 '스퀘어 마일'을 따로 떼어 내기 어렵다. 살아있는 박물관의 일부일 뿐.

박물관의 한 부분이 된 오래된 건물
A old building as a part of museum

Civic Centre like a museum dancing over time

Around half an hour by rain from Surbiton to Walterloo. It has a strange atmosphere with a distinct elegance thanks to the spatial juxtaposition of the City of London, known as the Square Mile, located in central London. While I am strolling along the stylish streets among elegant buildings between the cotton-cloudy sky and the land sprinkled with large and small stones, I often get a wide range of senses through the gentle scenery. When I walk along each street, my eyes' pupils dilate before the features: fitness of artifacts between water stream and hillslope, contrasting tension between the straight road and winding alleys, visual continuity of building walls, a juxtaposition between historical landmarks and modern skyscrapers, and so on. Riddles generated by spatial language!

When I stay at streets in the Square Mile area, I feel startled and excited despite the cold air. It is because many historical artifacts concerning the history of London have evolved over 2,000 years in the life world. The local atmosphere's unique sense is likely linked with the spirit of place cultivated and sustained by the citizens with nameless buildings and street furniture on the land below the vast sky. In addition to these senses, I also feel the primordial shape of the place through the gravel surface of the road that is transmitted to the plantar cells. Urban skins shaping time senses!

Because there are no vacant gaps between buildings, a street wall is mainly composed of buildings' frontages. When I stare at a street wall, although I do not know how much time has passed, I can try to infer from stories of the street's history through the surface of bricks or stones on the wall. In this civic centre, I am fascinated by the imagination that as time passed, the rich historical center became more and more museum. The Square Mile area seems to become a part of a museum of London. Even in my mind, I am no longer able to detach the Square Mile from London's museum. It is just a part of a vivid museum.

29th October

Where Newton, Charles Darwin, Stephen Hawking, and others are located, Westminster Abbey

건물 높이가 비슷하여 중심치역 가로벽

A street wall similar in height of buildings

나무들이 벽이 되는 줄지어 공원

A green wall similar in height of trees

하늘 빛이 희미해지는 잿빛 밤 다섯 시

밤이 길어짐에 따라 상상할 수 있는 세상은 점점 더 깊어지고 있다. 저녁 식사 후 나는 어쩔 수 없이 집에 머물러 방이 밝아 질 때까지 방을 돌아다닌다. 때로는 어두워지는 하늘과 뒷마당을 통해 나타나는 벽, 지붕 및 나무의 단조로운 실루엣을 본다. 그리고 화려한 하늘, 풍요로운 땅, 온화한 사람들, 시민을 위한 평화로운 성, 풀에 맺힌 투명한 이슬방울, 차분하게 울리는 노래 등.

내 마음이 꿈꾸는 왕국에서 어둠과 밝음의 가장자리 사이의 가장자리를 어떻게 상상할 수 있을까? 아마도 경계가 있다면 지금은 내게 맞닥뜨리는 이 시간의 끝이 바로 그 순간 인 것 같다. 방 안쪽이 밝아지는 동안 방 바깥쪽 빛이 어두워진다. 교회 시계탑 꼭대기에 걸려있는 종이 울리면 방의 투명함이 상상력이 넘치는 소리의 물결로 채워진다. 내 뇌 속의 깨어진 기억은 종소리와 함께 흔들리고 있다.

어둠 속의 하늘, 땅, 성, 시민 등의 상상의 그림은 현실에서는 어두워지지만 내 마음 속에는 꿈틀거린다. 환상의 본능적 기억에 이어진 마음은 빛나는 마음 거울에 비친 인상적인 그림을 드러낸다. 날카롭게 갈라진 존

168

재의 특징이 부드러워지고 갈라진 틈 사이의 가상의 이음이 마음 속 장면

을 거울처럼 비춘다. 명명되지 않은 존재들은 방을 통해 마음속에 명명된

존재로 스스로를 다시 만들고 있다.

마을에 있는 상징물, 시계탑

The clock tower, a symbol in Surbiton

5 o'clock at grey night when the skylight fades

As the nighttime is getting longer, the imageable world is getting deeper. After dinner, I am unavoidably staying inside my house and roam around the rooms until they become bright, with one and another imagination. Sometimes I see the darkening sky and the monotonous silhouette of the walls, roofs, and trees appearing through the backyard. And while I have wandered all over the rooms, I have been enjoying meeting with the beings that grant meaning to the kingdom of my mind, like the colorful sky, plentiful land, gentle people, peaceful castles for the citizen, transparent dewdrops on weeds, the placidly ringing song and so on.

How can I imagine a border between the edge of darkness and the edge of brightness in an ideal kingdom of my mind? Perhaps if there is a border, now this edge of time confronting me will seem to be just that moment. While the inside of the rooms is getting brighter, the glow of the outside of the rooms is getting darker. As the bell hanging at the top of a clock tower is ringing, the room's transparentness is filled with the imaginative wave of sound. The breaking memories in my brain are fluctuating with the tune of the bell sound.

The imaginary picture of sky, land, castle, citizen, etc., in the full darkness, is dimming in reality but wriggling in my mind. My mind, which is coupled with the phantasms' instinct memory, reveals an impressive picture reflected on a mirror of my illuminating mind. The features of the sharply split beings smoothen, and the imaginary bonding between the splits reflects the scene in mind as a mirror. The unnamed beings are reinventing themselves as named beings in mind over the rooms.

19th November

원형 교사도 주변
A roundabout surrounding area

"공주는 달 아래 지구에서 앎이 으뜸이라고 생각했다. 그녀는 먼저 모든 과학 배우기를 바랐고 그 다음 대학을 세우고 싶어 했다. 왕자는 정의(正義, Justice)를 잘 다스릴 수 있는 작은 왕국을 바랐다. 이믈락과 천문학자는 삶의 흐름에 따라 살고 싶어 했다."

"The princess thought, that of all sublunary things, knowledge was the best. She desired first to learn all sciences, and then purposed to found a college of learned women. ⋯ The prince desired a little kingdom, in which he might administer justice in his own person, and see all the parts of government with his own eyes. ⋯ Imlac and the astronomer were contented to be driven along the stream of life without directing their course to any particular port."

Samuel Johnson, *The History of Rasselas, Prince of Abissinia*, 2009 (Oxford University Press, The book was first published in April 1759 in England.)

밤 다섯 시 집 앞 마을 주차장
5 p.m., parking lot in front of the house

진실에 미치지 못하는 언어

뜻의 상징체계인 언어는 내 감성과 이성의 인식 일부를 걸러내는 것 같다. 사용할 때마다 마음의 왕국을 이끌고 경험하고 상상하는 세계로 넓히는 큰 뜻 상자이다. 최근까지 나는 언어에 어려움을 겪었다. 오늘 나는 언어에 또 속는다. 세상은 고정 관념에 빙 둘러싸여 있다. 이유가 만들어지면 감각이 일어난다. 인지할 수 있는 한 순간 나는 오랜 생각을 지우고 그 순간에 어울리는 새로운 생각을 가져온다. 감성과 이성 사이에 오해를 만드는 언어는 아이러니하다. 내 생각을 모호하게 한다.

오늘도 어제처럼 언어의 가장자리를 맴돌고 있다. 집의 창문을 열면 바람에 흩날리는 나뭇가지 소리가 들린다. 차가운 공기가 나뭇가지를 간지럽히는 것 같다. 여기 저기 거리에 많은 나뭇잎이 쌓여 있다. 나뭇잎이 더 가까이 오라고 손짓하는 것 같다. 지나가는 사람들이 나뭇잎을 밟고 있는 동안 나뭇가지가 쌀쌀한 공기와 함께 노니는 것 같다. 오늘 내 마음 속의 말은 나뭇가지에 나뭇잎과 함께 흔들리고 있다.

순간적인 마음 움직임을 어떻게 모두 드러낼까? 당황함, 공허함, 변덕스러움, 소동, 모호함 등. 나는 늘 언어 제약이 없는 끝없는 세상에 살고프

다. 언어를 넘어 모르는 세계를 상상한다. 언어는 감성과 이성을 공식화

된 세계로 계속 밀어 붙인다. 언어 상자에서 벗어나면 특별한 공간 경험

을 할 수 있을까? 겉이 어두워지고 속은 가벼워지는 사이 언어는 시시각

각 흔들린다. 감성과 이성이 함께.

말 없는 스케이트장
A silent skating rink

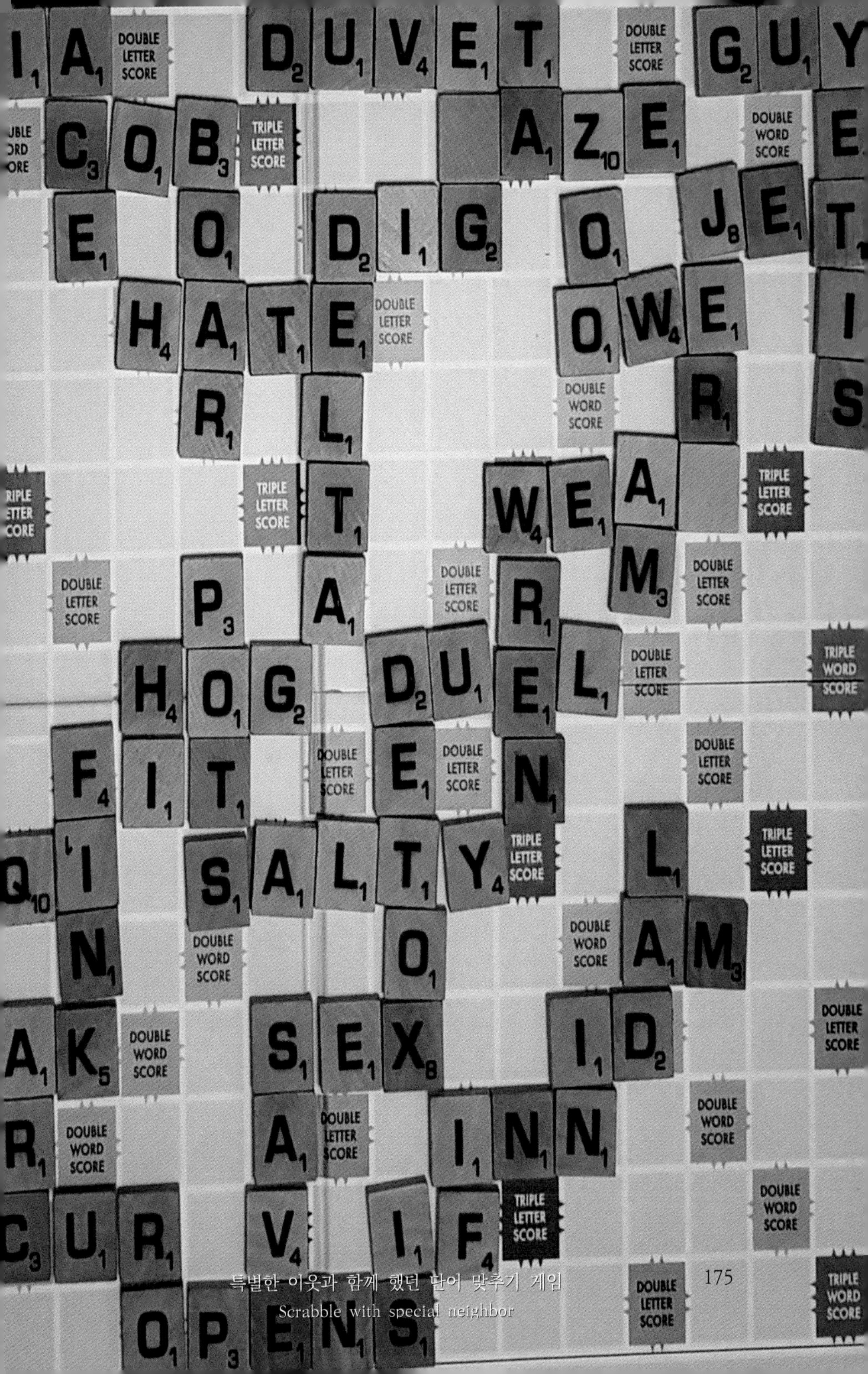

특별한 이웃과 함께 했던 단어 맞추기 게임
Scrabble with special neighbor

Language less than truth

As a symbolic system of meaning, language seems to filter out some of the perceptions of my sense and reason. At all moments, whenever I use it, I regard it as an extensive toolbox filled with meaning, inducing the kingdom of my mind to extend into the world I experience and imagine. Until recently, I have struggled with the language. Today, I was even cheated by language. The world I sense and the reason are enclosed by stereotypes, the fixed meaning of many words-sense rouses as the reason forms. For a moment, I can perceive, I erase an old idea, and I bring a new idea compatible with that moment. It is an irony that language makes various misconnection between sense and reason. It is because the language makes my thoughts vague.

Today like yesterday, I am hovering around the boundary of language. As I open the window in my house, I listen to the rustle of tree branches in the breeze. Chilly air seems to tickle the tree branches. Many leaves lay in heaps here and there on the street. The leaves seem to beckon me to come nearer. While passers-by are stepping on the leaves, the tree branches seem to play with the chilly air. Today, the words in my mind are shaking with the tree branches and the leaves together. I find I am muttering something to myself.

How can I wholly reveal a momentary fluctuation in my mind? There are many things: bewilderment, emptiness, capriciousness, tumult, dubiousness, vagueness, and so on. I always wish to live in a world of infinitude where there is no constraint of language. I imagine a genuine world I do not know, beyond the linguistic world. Tongue keeps pushing my sense and reason into a formalized world. Will I be able to have a unique experience in this space if I escape from the language toolbox? While the outside is getting darker and the inside is getting lighter, language is shaking with sense and reason from moment to moment.

26th November

말 없는 음악 연주
A musical performance without word

시간과 공간을 엮는 순간들

어렴풋이 반짝이는 물 위, 세상으로 꼬드긴 날들은 사라지고 낯선 날들이 느닷없이 번뜩인다. 기억에 눌어붙은 흐릿한 날들이 안개 속에 꿈틀거리며 마음 속 이러 저리 맴돈다. 마음과 세상 사이의 날들은 텅 빈 데로 흐르고 있다. 드러나지 않은 날들 사이에서 나는 그 움직임에 귀 기울이고 있다.

많은 날들이 마법의 세계로 흐르는 동안 템즈 강가 '기억 의자'에서 세상을 찬찬히 둘러본다. 나는 혼자이어야 하지만 그렇지 않다. 마음에 쌓인 날들은 여기로 쏟아져 나와 되살아난다. 날들이 잇따르고 시시각각 세상을 넘어 보이지 않는 시원(始原)의 배가 다가온다. 이 시간과 공간 사이에서 날들을 텅 빈 곳으로 보낸다. 날은 시간과 공간을 엮은 매듭이리라.

어디에나 날들이 있다. 그동안 얼마나 많은 날들을 이 곳에서 느꼈고 잊었는지 알지 못한다. 서서히 감각에 집중하고 마음을 넓게 연다. 내 감각과 기억에서 방황하는 날들을 다시 살려본다. 날들이 나를 감싸는 동안 혼자가 아니라는 것을 느낀다. 이곳을 떠난 후, 감각과 마음에 연결된 이 날들의 일부는 다른 사람을 기다리면서 남으리라.

잔잔한 물결과 우아한 백조
Gentle waves and elegant swans

Moments in-between time and space

On a vaguely twinkling water surface, the moments which coax me into sensing the world disappear, and unco moments suddenly appear in front of my mind like a bolt out of the blue. Uncertain moments cohering with my memories float aimlessly in my mind as they are hazily permeated into the air like a wriggling of mist. The moments between my mind and the world are flowing into the emptiness of the world. Between the moments unrevealed, I am pricking up the ears of my mind to perceive what the moments move.

While many moments empty themselves into a magic world, on a 'memorable bench' by Thames' riverside, I composedly look around my world near me again. I am supposed to be alone, but I am not. The moments stored in my mind pour out and revive in this place. There are other moments on the heels of the moments regenerating. From moment to moment, an invisible primordial boat beyond the world comes to me. I send the moments into the emptiness between this time and this space. A moment might be defined as a knot tangling up time and space.

There are infinite moments everywhere. In this place, I do not know totally how many moments have been perceived and lost during the past year. I slowly concentrate on my sense and widely open my mind. I regenerate moments wandering in my sense and memory. While I am here, I perceive I am not alone while I cover myself with moments. After I leave this place, a part of the moment connecting my sense and mind will remain, waiting for someone else to come.

4th December

※ 이 글은 나의 연수 보고서인 '런던의 중심지 재생 경험이 주는 함의'에도 실었다.

This essay was also published in my oversea report, "The Implications of the Regeneration Experience on the urban centres in London"

"새로운 도시에 다다라 텅 빈 거리를 이리저리 돌아다니는 것에는 무언가 특별한 게 있지. 그 다다름에 대한 사랑을 절대 잃지 않으려 하겠지만 그래도 난 떠날 운명인 걸."
"There's something about arriving in new cities, wandering empty streets with no destination. I will never lose the love for the arriving, but I'm born to leave." Charlotte Eriksson, *Empty Roads & Broken Bottles: in search for The Great Perhaps*

하늘, 숲, 땅, 그리고 사람
Sky, forest, land, water and human

184

우주와의 만남 (邂逅)

Encounter with the universe

"참 낯섦을 바라다"

TOWARD THE TRUE STRANGENESS

지구에서 살아가는 느낌
Sense of living on earth

Beauty of a long time

지금 그 '느낌'에 대해서

어떤 공간에서 낯섦을 느끼는 경험은 옥살이 같은 어떤 규칙의 공간에서 벗어났다는 뜻일 수도 있다. 언어를 뛰어 넘는 느낌을 불러일으키는 낯섦은 존재에 대해 스스로에게 질문을 던진다. 모르면 몰라도 낯섦은 내가 여기 살아 있다는 증거에 관한 어떤 것이리라. 내가 스스로 살아있다는 것을 확인하기란 쉽지 않기 때문이다.

낯섦이 세면 셀수록 삶의 근원에 대한 물음도 커지는 것 같다. 살고 있던 곳과 많이 다른 곳에 갑자기 준비 없이 몸이 놓이게 될 때 낯섦은 보다 세게 느껴진다. 시간이 지날수록 낯선 곳에 대한 느낌의 세기는 그 첫 느낌의 세기보다 낮아지지만 다시 기존의 익숙했던 곳으로 돌아오면 그 낯선 느낌의 강도가 다시 높아진다. 익숙했던 곳이 반갑게 낯설기만 하다.

런던을 떠나 이년이 지난 후, 나는 그 날 그 판과 함께 지금 부산에서 지내고 있다. 삼백 육십 삼일 동안 낯선 공간에서 그 날 그 판이 모양 지었던 그 느낌은 내 몸 속 어딘가에서 이러 저리 돌아다니고 있는 듯하다. 어느 겨울 날 템즈강 가 햄프튼 코트 산책길에서 따갑게 이마를 때리던 추위는 아직도 내 이마 주위 어딘가 즈음에서 맴돌고 있다. 어느 여름 날

뒷마당에서 창문을 넘어 온 상쾌한 바람은 여전히 내 피부 주위에서 잠잔다.

조금만 그 시간과 공간을 떠올려 보면 몸은 늘 그 느낌을 불러올 태세다. 가끔씩 불러오려 하지만 그 느낌이 이 느낌이, 이 느낌이 그 느낌이 아니니 별 수는 없다. 어떤 느낌이 그 느낌이었는지 헷갈린다. 그것들 중의 일부는 내 몸 어딘가에 꼭꼭 숨어 버린 것인가? 아니면 어디로 달아나 버린 것인가? 손과 발바닥부터 몸 전체의 살갗과 근육, 그리고 뇌에 새긴 그 날 그 판이 흐릿하다. 갑자기 그 날 그 판이 낯설게 성큼 다가온다.

이 글을 쓴지 얼마나 지났을까? 가족이 앉아 얼굴을 마주하기도 하고 노트북을 펼쳐 놓았던 허름한 밝은 갈색 나무 식탁과 의자, 겨울밤에 흰 창문을 통해 들려온 작은 나뭇가지 부딪히는 소리, 학교에서 돌아온 딸이 뛰어내리던 버스 정류장, 아내와 함께 앉아있던 공원 의자 앞을 이러 저리 내달리던 다람쥐, 동네 한가운데 서있던 뾰족한 콘크리트 시계탑, 템즈 강가 잔디 위에 앉아 햄프튼 코트 위 노을을 바라보며 먹던 피자 등 그 느낌들이 갑자기 몸 전체에서 다시 샘솟기 시작한다. 그 날 그 판이 이 날 이 판으로 다시 그려진다.

2021.1.2

냉이처럼 가지를 뻗은 민들레
A shepherd's purse-like dandelion

On the metasense now

The experience of "strangeness" in space may mean that I have escaped from a space of rules, such as a prison. The "strangeness," which evokes a sense beyond language, asks me a question about human existence. If my guess is correct, the notion of strangeness is something concerning the evidence that I am alive. Because it is not easy for me to prove that I am alive on my own.

The stronger the strength of the strangeness, the greater the question of life's source seems to grow. When I suddenly place my body from a familiar environment to an unfamiliar environment, the 'strangeness' feels stronger. Over time, the intensity of the sense of strangeness becomes less intense than the intensity of the first sense, but when I return to a familiar place, the intensity of the sense of strange increases again. I realized that familiar places are pleasantly strange.

Two years after leaving London, I am now living in Busan with the moments and the fields experienced at Surbiton in

London. The senses that the moments and the fields were shaped in the strange space for 363 days two years seem to be moving around somewhere in my body. On a winter's day, the sharp cold on my forehead on the Hampton Court promenade along the Thames river still seems to linger somewhere around my forehead. One summer day, the refreshing breeze from the backyard through the window is still sleeping around my skin.

When I recall the time and the space I experienced at Surbiton in London, I perceive that my body is always poised to bring the senses with me. I try to bring those up sometimes, but I can't do that soundly because those senses are not these senses and these senses are not those senses. I'm confused about what kind of senses those were. Did some of the senses hide well somewhere in my body? If not, where do they run away? From the soles of the hands and feet to the skin and muscles of the whole body and the brain, they seem that the moments and the fields are hazy. Suddenly, the moments and the senses come to me strangely and quickly.

How long has it been since I wrote this article? The shabby light brown wooden dining table and chairs with laptops spread out for the family to sit face to face, the sound of bumping small branches through a white window on a winter night, the bus stop where the daughter returned from school jumped. The squirrel running around in front of the bench in the park where I sat with my wife, the pointed concrete clock tower standing in the middle of the town, and the pizza I ate while watching the sunset on the Hampton Court sitting on the grass by the river Thames, all of a sudden the senses restart to spring up from my whole body. Those moments and those fields are depicted again as these moments and these fields.

January 2021

약 천백 년 전인 925년에 지어진 '모든 성자들의 교회'
All Saints Church, built in 925, about one thousand hundred years ago

낯선 **내일**이길 바라는 말

한 사람이 떠오른다. 이교도로 몰린 그녀, 테스는 '나는 고향에 온 거나 마찬가지예요.'라고 말했다. 토마스 하디(Thomas Hardy)가 쓴 소설, 「더 빌가의 테스(Tess of D'Urbervilles)」. 스톤헨지에서 밤을 지낸 뒤, 죽기에 앞서 그녀가 남긴 말이다. 그녀에게 이곳은 낯선 돌무더기 터가 아니라 따뜻한 집 같은 느낌의 자리가 아니었을까? 아이러니하게도 그 때 '이교도의 신전(神殿)'으로 인식되던 이곳은 세상의 편견으로 죽게 된 테스의 따뜻한 고향이 되었다. 어쩌면 태어나 자란 그곳보다 더 따스한 그 느낌이 춤을 추는 낯선 이곳에서.

테스가 어쩌면 낯선 스톤헨지에서 솔즈베리 들판을 보며 느꼈을 그 느낌이란 무엇일까? 토마스 울프(Thomas Wolfe)가 「그대 다시는 고향에 못 가리(You can't go home again)」에 그려낸 조지도 불러와 본다. 낯선 타향살이를 뒤로 하고 늘 그리워하던 고향으로 돌아왔건만 차가워진 사람들 얼굴과 망가진 마을 모습에 낯설게 마주한 한 사람, 조지. 고향에 끝내 가지 못한 소설 속 주인공처럼 나도 마찬가지이리라. 고향은 시간과 공간에 얽매인 고달픈 떠돌이 삶을 달래는 꿈일 뿐인 것일까?

참 삶은 세상에 쳐놓은 인식의 그물에 물음들을 쉼 없이 던진다. 시간과 공간에 삶이 엮이면 세상의 질서는 이리저리 으스러져 흩어지고 만다. 시간은 '날줄'로 공간은 '판줄'로 그 가장 자리가 엷어져 뒤섞여 버린다. 한 줄기 날파람과 실구름의 만남처럼 그 그물은 불현듯 사라지고 나는 낯선 세상 속으로 빠져들고 만다. 그도 내 그 느낌과 닮았었던가? 토마스 만 (Thomas Mann)은 「마의 산(The Magic Mountain)」속, 한스 카스트로프의 낯선 경험들을 통해 시간에 대한 고정관념을 와르르 무너뜨린다. '시간은 지나감을 나타낼 눈금이 없지. 새 달이나 새 해의 시작을 알리는 큰 나팔소리도 없어. 세기가 시작되더라도 총을 쏜다거나 종을 울린다든지 하는 것은 우리 인간들뿐이야.'

한드케 (P. Handka)는 그의 소설, 「느린 귀향(Slow Homecoming)」에서 지질학자 소저를 통해 '삶의 순간들'을 상상력으로 다시 맞출 필요가 있다고 했다. 삶에서 펼쳐지는 인식은 한계를 드러내고 기존 인식의 가장 자리를 넘어가 버린다. 고정관념의 그물로 형성된 세상의 기존 인식을 넘어 시원 (始元)에 대해 묻는다. 낯선 세상에서 참과 마주한 사람, 공자가 물가에 앉아 흐르는 물을 보며 이리 말했던가? '흘러가는 것이 이러하구나 (逝者如斯夫: 서자여사부), 밤낮을 머물지 않으니 (不舍晝夜, 불사주야),' 얼마나 비워내야 하리 풀어내야 하리. 노자는 '도를 도라 부르면 참 도가 아니요, 말로 드러낼 수 있으면 참 존재가 아니다 (道可道 非常道 名可名 非相名; 도가도 비상도 명가명 비상명),'라고 하지 않았던가? 내가 늘 깨어있기 위해서는 세상이 늘 낯설어야 할지도 모르겠다.

어린이가 읽는 동화지만, 영모 이야기는 나에게 흥미롭게 다가온다. 공지희는 「영모가 사라졌다」에서 현실과 이어진 다른 세상을 신비롭고 낯설게 그린다. 병구는 집 나간 단짝 친구, 영모를 찾기 위해 고양이를 따라 담벼락 너머 낯선 '제온제나 (즐거움을 뜻하는 제온과 스스로의 참 나를 뜻하는 제나가 합쳐진 우리말)' 세상에 마주한다. 시공간의 뒤틀림 속, 두 세상에서 스스로를 발견해 가는 날과 판 이야기를 그린다. 이 이야기는 나에게 담벼락 안쪽의 고정관념을 넘어선 상상의 날개를 꿈틀거리게 한다. 참 세상을 향해 혐상 (嫌像, Dystopia)과 이상, 실상과 환상, 오늘과 내일 사이에 낯선 담벼락이 필요함을 느낀다. 그 담벼락 위에서 신비로운 세상에 낯선 궁금증을 던지고 풀어야 하리.

'감히, 아름답다'라고 밖에 말하기 어려운 참 살이 이야기. 섬진강 평사리 마을에서 간도 (間島)에 이르는 무수한 그 날 그 판 이야기에 천착한 박경리의 「토지 (土地)」가 화살이 되어 마음에 꽂힌다. 그녀는 특수한 시공

196

간 속에서 굴곡진 삶을 살아갈 수밖에 없는 수많은 사람들의 삶을 우주적 스케일로 그려낸다. 정말 많은 사람들이 이루는 날과 판이 줄줄 나와 숭고한 파노라마가 된다. 저마다 간직한 시공간의 날과 판 이야기들은 시공간의 가장자리를 넘어 끊임없이 꿈틀댄다. 이 날과 판이 이루는 우주적 시원에 대한 근원적 물음은 아마 지구에서 최고봉이 아닐까도 싶다. '눈물 때문에 서희 모습이 물감처럼 번져 나간다'하니 그 날과 판의 이음새가 물들고, '속박에서 풀려나오는 순간 공허가 밀려온다. 공허 속에 어둠이 스며오고, 밤의 고요함이 아프게 가슴을 훑고 지나간다'하니 그 마디가 스르륵 풀려버린다.

소설은 어디까지나 소설이다. 글로 지은 상상의 세상은 나에게 기존 인식의 가장자리를 넘어 낯선 세상을 마음껏 만끽하게 하고 익숙한 현실을 낯설게 보이게 한다. 하지만 상상은 상상에 머문다. 삶의 시원에 대한 물음으로 가는 길을 낸 「토지」는 그 마저 훌쩍 뛰어 넘어가려 하지만. 참 세상은 틀림없이 이보다 더 어림잡기 어렵다. 글 너머에 존재하는 어떤 느낌을 이루는 '날줄'과 '판줄'이 움직이니 그럴 수밖에. 이 세상은 모든 사람들이 등장하거니와 각자가 주인공이 되어야하기 때문이다.

세상은 아주 작은 먼지 한 톨, 흙 알갱이, 돌멩이, 이슬 한 방울, 작은 씨앗, 풀, 나뭇잎, 보도블록, 벽돌, 가로등, 의자, 우체통, 건물, 구조물, 마을, 도시, 지구, 우주, 다른 세상까지 아우른다. 알려진 대로 이들을 이러 저리 재는 단위가 작게는 10^{-24}를 뜻하는 '욕토 (yocto)'에서 크게는 10^{24}를 뜻하는 '요타 (yotta)'까지 이른다. 길이는 '욕토미터 (ym)'에서 '요타미터 (Ym)'까지이며 무게는 '욕토그램 (yg)'에서 '요타그램 (Ym)'까지이다. 그러나 이 단위는 그저 눈금일 뿐이다.

이미 말한 것처럼, 나는 세상에서 사람이 느낄 수 있는 가장 작은 시간 단위는 '날줄'이요, '판줄'은 가장 작은 공간 단위로 이름 지었다. 무엇인가에 이름을 짓는 찰나, 그 것이 이미 아닐 수 있다는 옛 사람의 말씀처럼 이 두 줄이 무엇인지, 그리고 작용으로 이루어지는 그 느낌이 어떤 실체인지 아직 잘 모른다. 상상 실험을 해 보았을 때, 모두 비운 방에서는 '날줄'과 '판줄'의 움직임이 없으므로 그 느낌이 있을 수 없다. 거꾸로 채운 방이 있다 하면 그것이 드러날까? 그 느낌은 이 두 줄이 따로 움직이는 게 아니라 함께 해서 생기는 것 같다. 누구라도 좀 더 많은 사람이 좀 더 나은 삶을 살기 바란다면 그 실체에 가깝게 다가가는 노력이 필요하리라. 왜 그리고 무엇으로 그 느낌을 자세히 할 수 있을까? 쉽게 느낄 수 있는 밝음과 어두움, 차가움과 뜨거움부터 형식적인 아름다움과 못남을 비롯하여 설명하기 어려운 도취(陶醉 Euphoria), 숭고(崇高, Sublime), 정의(正義, Justice), 도덕(道德, Morality)에 이르기까지. 말로 담기 어려운 세상의 '날줄'과 '판줄'이 이루는 그 느낌을 어떻게 풀어 매어야 하는가?

낯설게 다가온 그 느낌을 알 수 있다면 세상을 그만큼 더 헤아릴 수 있을게다. '날줄'과 '판줄'이 함께 움직여 이루어지는 그 '참 느낌'은 넓고 깊은 앎이 있어야 어느 정도 깨달을 수 있으려나. 어쩌면 나름대로 쌓아온 앎 모두를. 사람 세상을 이해하는 철학, 심리학, 뇌과학, 생물학, 인류학 등을 알아야 할지 모른다. 게다가 우주 속 물리 세상을 이해하기 위해 물리학, 지리학, 지질학, 천문학, 우주학 등도 이어야 한다. 사람이 만든 공간 세상은 건축학, 조경학, 토목학, 도시학, 전기·전자학, 기계학 등이 이어진다. '참 느낌'의 실체는 기존 앎의 다시 맞춤과 넓힘으로 좀 더 드러나리라. 쪼개진 기존 앎 간추림! 기존 앎 모두를 알고 다루기 어려워 보이지만 어딘가에 풀 실마리가 있으리라. 이도 저도 아닌 느낌의 번짐을 막을 수 있는 세상을 꿈꾸어 본다.

모든 앎이 시공간에서 함께 다루어질 때, 그 '참 느낌'에 대한 실체에 가깝게 다가갈 수 있으리라. 예부터 이어져 내려온 우리 세계관인 사람(나와 남)을 널리 도우라는 뜻의 '홍익인간(弘益人間)'을 바탕으로 우주를

아울러 '인문우주학 (人文宇宙學)'이라고 크게 정리하면 어떨까 싶다. 최한기의 '기학 (氣學)', 김용옥의 '민본성 (民本性, Pletharchia)', 에드워드 홀의 '공간인류학 (空間人類學)', 데이비드 그레이버의 '자주인 인류학 (自主人人類學, Anarchist Anthropology) 등도 참조할만하다. 앎 밝히기가 빨라지고 인공지능이 나아지고 있어 곧 알 수 있을 것 같기도 하다. 그 첫 앎의 얼개를 '느낌학'이라 부르면 어떨까? 드러난 모두를 다루는 '경관학'도 괜찮다. 아니면 보다 적극적으로, 살아 움직이는 관계 모두가 그리는 아름다움인 '동미학 (動美學, Kinaesthetics)'이라고 해보면 어떨까도 싶다. 에드워드 홀은 '근접공간학 (近接空間學, Proxemics)'이라고 이름 지었던가? 결국, 그것은 내가 아니더라도 누군가에 의해 무엇이든지 되겠지만.

몸이 힘드니 거꾸로 마음은 자유로워진다. 이 글은 더 좋은 내일을 일구라는 뜻으로 내가 나 스스로에게 주는 보약이다. 부디 아프지 말길. 거짓을 모양 짓는 모두가 사라지길. 따뜻한 마음으로 끝없는 세상 속에서 그리운 고향을 일구는 낯선 한 사람의 나이길 바란다.

매암산 아래에서

특별한 이웃인 칼슨 교수와 그의 가족에게 마음 깊이 감사드린다.

검은 의자에서   On the black bench

마음 실타래 기억 무덤에 푸니,   The skein of my heart into the memory tomb,
하늘 빛 깨어나 땅 빛 잠드나?   The sky opens, the land sleeps?
빛에 모양 주는 구름은   Clouds shape the light
바람 그러모아 내닫고   They gather up the winds, fade away

돌이 땅에 그린 시간 무늬   Stones portray the time orders on the land
결이 물에 뿌린 땅 그림자   Shadows of ground sown in water
내 빛줄기 어디에 있나?   Where is a ray of light?
길 따라 여닫는 흐릿한 우주   A blurry universe floating along the street

빛이 벼리는 살갗 아래   Under the glowing skin surface
바람이 내린 한 빛 줄기   A light streaming from the wind
들풀 이파리 하늘로 피어   Wild-grassed leaves facing the sky
흔드는 날과 판, 춤사위 !   Dancing, just with moments and fields !

누구에게는 성지, 누구에게는 고향, 누구에게는 관광지로 불리는 스톤 헨지
Stonehenge, called a holy place for some, hometown for some, and tourist destination for some.

What I wish for myself toward a strange tomorrow

A person called a pagan comes to mind. Tess said, 'I feel like I come back to my hometown.' The novel, "Tess of D'Urbervilles," written by Thomas Hardy. After spending the night at the ancient site of Stonehenge, she left her words before her death. Maybe this was not a place with strange stones for her, but a warm house? Ironically, this place, which was known as a 'pagan temple' at the time, became a warm house for Tess, who had to die because of the prejudice of the world. Maybe in a strange place where the true sense, which is warmer than the place where she was born and raised, dances.

What was the true sense she would have felt at the strange Stonehenge, seeing the fields of Salisbury? I also recall George, who appears in Thomas Wolfe's novel, "You Can't Go Home Again." George, who has returned to his home he has always missed but strangely faces the chilled temperament of people and the broken home landscape. Like the protagonist in the novel who can't go to his home, I will be the same. Is the home just a dream of comforting a struggling wandering life tied to time and space?

True life constantly throws questions into the net of the stereotype that has been laid in the world. When true life is intertwined with time and space, the world's order is crushed around and scattered. Time is replaced by 'momentome (naljul in Korean)' and space is replaced by 'fieldome (panjul in Korean),' and the edges are blurred and mixed. Like the meeting of a gust of wind and a thin thread-like cloud, the net suddenly disappears and I fall into a strange world. Did he look like my sense? Thomas Mann breaks down the stereotype of time through Hans Castrop's bizarre experiences in "The Magic Mountain." 'Time has no divisions to mark its passage. There is never a thunderstorm or blare of trumpets to announce the beginning of a new month or year. Even when a new century begins, it is only we mortals who ring bells and fire off pistols.'

In his novel, "Slow Homecoming," P. Handka said that he needed to re-imaginate the moments of life through geologist Sorger.

Perceptions that permeate into life reveal limitations and go beyond the edge of existing perceptions. He asks about the primordial impulses beyond the existing perception of the world formed by a net of stereotypes. So, did Confucius, who faced the truth in a strange world, sat down by a stream and said to his disciples? 'This is what goes on. Water passes day and night without staying.' When true life permeates the net of time and space, a passage to the true universe seems to open up. How much do I have to empty my mind and how do I have to refine my mind? Lao-tzu said that if someone calls 'tao' as 'tao,' it is not a true 'tao,' and that if someone reveals something with words, the true being concerning something gets trapped in the word. The world may always have to be strange to me to be awake all the time.

The story of Youngmo, the main character in the fairy tale, also comes to me interestingly. In "Seasons in Another World," Gong Ji-hee describes in detail a mysterious and strange world connected to reality. Byeonggoo faces the strange world of 'Xeonzena (a

Korean word that combines Xeon meaning joy and Zena meaning true self)' over the wall along the cat to find his best friend, Youngmo, who left the house. In the twisted time and space, she describes the moments and fields of finding the true self in both worlds. This story gives me a wriggle of imaginary wings beyond the stereotypes inside the wall. To the true world, I feel the need for a strange wall between dystopia and utopia, reality and fantasy, today and tomorrow. On the wall, I have to ask strange questions about a mysterious world and solve the mystery that pops out of it.

It is difficult to describe, except for the sublime beauty. "The land", a novel written by Park Kyung-ni that contains numerous stories from Pyeongsari village next to the Seomjin River to Gando, seems to permeate my mind like an arrow. She truly portrays the lives of many who were forced to live twisted lives in special times and spaces, like the cosmic scale. It becomes a sublime panorama with a lot of people's moments and fields. The stories of people made by the moments and the fields constantly wriggle beyond the edge of time and space. The fundamental question of the cosmic origin of the moments and the fields is probably the highest peak on Earth. When I read, 'Seo-hee's tears spread like watercolor paints,' the knot woven with the moment and the field is stained. And the knot is loosened when I read, 'the moment I get out of my bondage, the darkness seeps into the emptiness, the calm of the night goes through my heart sorely.'

Novels are just novels. The imaginary world made by writing makes me feel the strange world beyond the edge of existing perception and makes the familiar reality seem strange. However, imagination is only in imagination. 'The land,' which made the way to the question for the primordial form of life, surpasses even that. The true world is undoubtedly more difficult to understand than this imaginary world. It is bound to become the true world because the 'momentome' and 'fieldome' that make up ambiguous senses that exist beyond literary works move. The real world is because everyone appears, and each person has to be the protagonist.

The true world is connected to everything, whether it is revealed or not. For example, from tiny dust, soil grains, stones, dew drops, small seeds, grass, tree leaves, bricks, street lights, chairs, buildings, structures, etc., to villages, cities, earth, space, and another world. As far as it is known, the units of these physical things range from 'yocto' to 'yotta.' The length is from 'ym (yocto meter)' to 'Ym (yotta meter)' and the weight is from 'yg (yocto gram)' to 'Ym (yotta gram).' However, these units have little to do with the sense.

As I explained earlier, I suggested that the smallest time units that a person can truly sense in the real world are the 'momentome,' and the 'fieldome' is the smallest space unit. Like the words of oriental philosophers, who said 'the moment I name something, the something doesn't become a true being,' I don't know what the two are and what the 'metasense (neucqim in Korean)' is. When I have experimented in my imagination, there is no the 'metasense' because there is no movement of 'momentome' and 'fieldome' in a complete room of emptiness. Assuming that there is a filled room, will the 'metasense' reveal its existence? I guess the 'metasense' is not caused by the two moving separately, but by acting together. If anyone wants more people to live in a better space, it is necessary to try to reach the reality of the 'metasense.' How is it possible? What can shape the true sense? From brightness and darkness, coldness and hotness to euphoria, sublime, morality, justice, which is difficult to explain. How can I understand the spatial literacy of a world that is difficult to express in words?

If I can know the ambiguous sense that has come to me strangely, I will be able to understand the true world better. The 'metasense,' which seems to be made up of the interaction of 'momentome' and 'fieldome,' will be able to understand to some extent by knowing many related academic parts. I need to learn philosophy, psychology, medical science, brain science, biology, anthropology, etc. that understand the human world. Physics, geography, geology, astronomy, cosmology, and so on should also be used to understand the physical world in the universe. The spatial world created by humankind is related to archaeology, architecture, landscape studies, civil engineering, urban science, electricity & electronics, mechanics and so on. I think the reality of 'metasense' will be revealed through the reconstruction of existing academic parts. Perhaps the starting point would be to experiment with my inner world. The grand reconstruction of the fragmented existing knowledge! It looks tough to know all of them, but there may be a clue somewhere. I dream of a world that can prevent the spread of 'dull sense' hang in the wind on Earth.

I think that all disciplines should be dealt with in time and space so that I approach the reality of 'metasense.' I wish to summarize various disciplines as the scientific relationship between humans and the universe based on the thought of 'hongik human (弘益人間, maximum service to humanity)' as the long-standing traditional thought in Korea. It is also worthy of reference to 'Hanki Choi's 'kihag (氣學),' Young-Oak Kim's 'pletharchia (民本性),' Edward Hall's 'anthropology of space,' David Graeber's 'anarchist anthropology' and so on. I expect that the degree of human knowledge accumulation will be rapidly increasing and artificial intelligence-based science and technology will be rapidly developing and become possible soon. What if the starting point for 'Humanities-Space Science' is called 'metasensitics (chamneucqim-hak in Korean)'? The landscape studies of dealing with everything that is revealed in the universe is also fine. Or, I would like to say, 'kinaesthetics,' which means all the beauty that is more active and moving. I guess that Edward T. Hall had called it 'proxemics.' After all, it will be done by someone.

As my body is getting harder, my mind is getting free. This book is the self-medicating method I prescribed for myself to shape a better tomorrow! Please don't be sick, and I hope that everything that shapes falsehood will break away from me. I hope I will become a ray of light that illuminates the infinite world and become a stranger who creates the true home for everyone in the real world.

April 2021

In my home under Maeam mountain, Busan

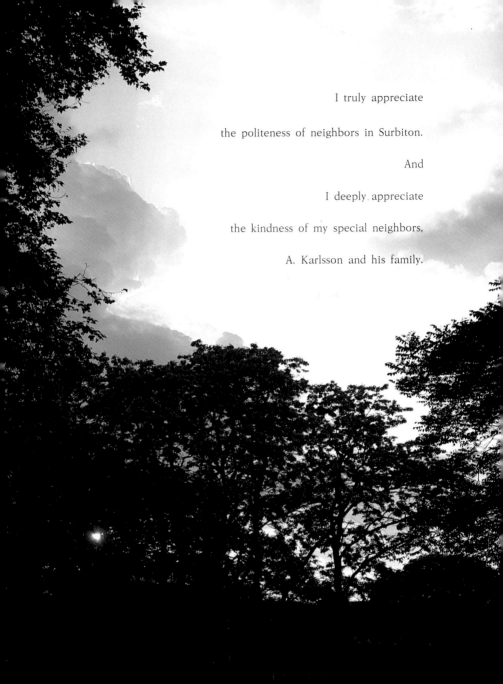

I truly appreciate

the politeness of neighbors in Surbiton.

And

I deeply appreciate

the kindness of my special neighbors,

A. Karlsson and his family.

빛이 들던 어느 날 거리에서
One day when the sun shined on me on the road

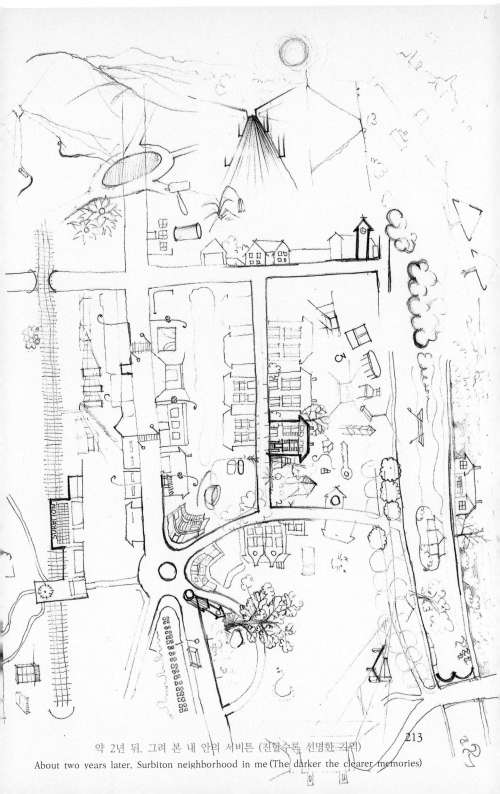

약 2년 뒤, 그려 본 내 안의 서비튼 (진할수록 선명한 기억)
About two years later, Surbiton neighborhood in me (The darker the clearer memories)

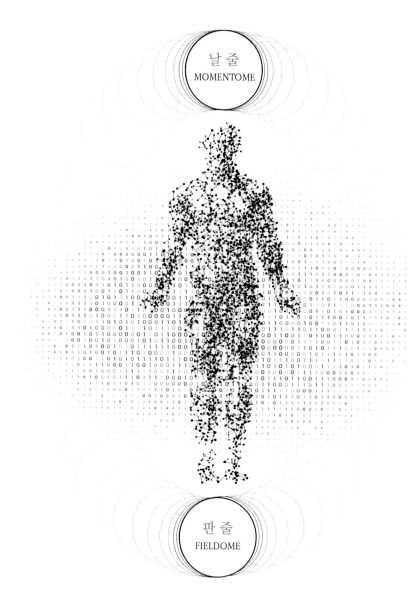

'날줄'과 '판줄'이 만나 이루는 동미학적 인간을 모양 지은 그림

The kinaesthetic human being concerning the 'Momentome' and the 'Fieldome' to sense the true world

Note: 이것은 두 디자인 자료를 가지고 한 작업 (This is based on two design materials)
Source: Materials designed by Starline and Vilmosvarga / Freepik

박상필 박사

나는 스스로를 늘 생각하며 지금 이 사랑스러운 지구에 살고 있다. 내가 살고 있는 이 고향 (모든 곳이 고향이라고 생각한다)을 보다 올바르게 살만한 곳으로 가꾸기 위해 무엇을 해야 할지 이리저리 애쓰는 궁금증 많은 나그네이다. 삶의 공간이 이루는 이야기라면 모두에 관심을 두고 있다. 꿈이 여전히 크다.

Ph.D., Sangphil Park

I live on this lovely planet now, and I am always thinking about who I am (I think all places are home).
I am a curious wanderer wondering what to do to make the planet a better place for everyone to live. I am interested in everything about the landscape that the relationship between time and space creates. I live with a sublime wish for the true world.

scapevalue@naver.com

런던에 있는 집 떠나기 며칠 전
A few days before I left my house in Surbiton, London